1

"*S*o tell me about your friends. What are they like?" I pressed on the brake to halt my minivan at the stoplight and glanced at my sister-in-law, Desi, who was riding in the passenger seat. We were on our way to meet with a client of the Boathouse Event Center, who happened to be a friend of Desi's.

"It's been a while, but back in college we all had a lot of fun together. Becca and I were roommates for our freshman and sophomore years at the University of Washington. Then we moved into a house off-campus for the last two years. Lindsay was a friend of Becca's from high school and rented a room in the house too." Desi looked thoughtful. "I haven't kept up with the rest of them very well. Becca and I do chat online sometimes, but I was a little surprised when she asked me to be a bridesmaid, much less the matron of honor." She shrugged.

"So how did Lindsay and Becca meet their significant others? They were part of your group too, right?" The light changed to green and I hit the gas. Desi and I were on our way to Becca's family's lake house, where most of the wedding party was staying.

"That's a funny story, actually. Lindsay was dating Bill, but when he met Becca, he only had eyes for her. They've been together ever since, but only recently decided to tie the knot."

"That doesn't sound too funny for Lindsay." I turned off on a smaller blacktop road, following the curves as they wound through grassy fields and wooded forests. In town, most of the grass had turned brown from the August heat, but out here the shade from the trees had kept everything green.

"Well, I suppose it wasn't," Desi admitted. "But she got over it quickly. We always teased her that she set them up. Anyways, it doesn't matter. She met her husband, Declan, through Bill, and they were married right after Lindsay graduated. Now, Bill, Declan, and another friend are partners in a dentistry office in Seattle."

"Hmm. I guess it did work out." I kept my eyes on the road, searching for the marker for Lake Elinor. "Did we miss the turnoff?"

She peered out the window. "I don't think so, but maybe? It's been so long since I was last out here. We used to come out in the summers to swim and water ski in the lake." She tapped on the window. "Jill, I think that's it, coming up by that grove of trees."

I slowed the car, eyeing the street sign before turning off. Lake Elinor Road. Sure enough, we'd finally found it. There weren't any public parks on the lake and I'd only been out here once before, for a party at the lake house of someone Adam worked with. Forty minutes out of town, Lake Elinor was far enough away that it felt like a vacation spot, but close enough for easy access to the city. Underneath the tires, the broken pavement crunched and we bounced in and out of potholes.

"They sure don't spend much on maintenance for this road," I grumbled.

"I think it's owned by the Lake Elinor Homeowner's Association, not the county."

Out of the corner of my eye, I saw Desi glance at the driving instructions in her lap.

"It says to take the first right onto Forrest Street and then a left onto Canary Road."

I dutifully followed her directions. Down the hill, the lake gleamed in the late summer sunlight. It wasn't a giant lake, but plenty big enough for water skiing fun and fishing.

"I think it's the brown house over there on the lakefront." Desi consulted the piece of paper.

"Which one?" At least half the houses on the lake were painted brown.

"The one with the three decks."

I pulled into the driveway behind a BMW, a Mercedes, and an Audi. A new-model truck with a boat trailer attached was parked on the side of the house. My Toyota Sienna rarely saw the inside of a car wash, but now I wished I'd taken more care to present a professional appearance. These might be Desi's friends, but they were also clients of mine and I wanted to make a good impression.

We got out of the car and stretched our legs. To take my mind off my not-so-clean minivan, I checked out the house. It was bigger than it appeared from afar. Judging by the mix of housing styles surrounding the lake, I doubted it had been the original structure. It was three stories tall and built in the Northwest contemporary style, with two tall, exposed wooden beams holding up a sharply V-shaped roofline. On one side of Becca's house was a small cabin with a tiny dock. On the other side was an ultramodern towering glass monstrosity that made the house we were visiting look middle-class.

The door opened before Desi and I managed to make it up the front steps. A Chihuahua wearing a bright-pink collar poked its nose out from behind the door. It looked so much like a large rat that I reflexively stepped back.

"Desi, you made it," cried an Asian woman in her early thirties. "Tilly, you can't go out there." She nudged the dog back inside and closed the door before running up to Desi and wrapping her arms around her. Desi returned the hug and then the woman stepped back, regarding my sister-in-law closely. "You haven't changed a bit."

"Right." Desi grinned. "I have a four-year-old and a baby. I don't exactly look like I did in college." She stared ruefully at the small pudge that rose above the waistline of her dark denim jeans.

"Oh, stop," the woman said, waving her hand at Desi. "You look great. And I loved those baby pictures you posted online. Lina is so gorgeous. I can't believe Anthony is four already though. We've got to get together sometime soon so I can meet both of them. It seems like the years are just flying by."

She seemed to finally notice me. "And is this Jill?" She stretched her hand out and I shook it. "I'm Becca Liu, Desi's friend from college."

"Yes, hi. I'm Jill. We spoke on the phone, but it's so nice to meet you in person." I smiled at her. She seemed very down-to-earth for coming from a family that, based on their vacation home, wasn't hurting for money.

"Nice to meet you too. I was sad to hear that Desi's mom

wasn't able to be here for our rehearsal dinner at the Boathouse, but it's nice to meet some more of the family. I'm happy Beth is taking some time off to visit her sister in Portland."

I nodded. "She deserves a break. She's had some health problems and I'm glad she's finally taking a break. This has been a very busy summer." I tried to sound confident, but inside, my stomach was twisting into knots. This was a big wedding and I needed to make sure everything was perfect for the rehearsal dinner and main event. Beth had put me in charge of managing things while she was gone but, luckily, she'd be back in time for the wedding next week.

Becca turned to Desi. "Are you going to be able to spend the night? My dad leaves on a business trip this Thursday and is gone for over a week, so I scheduled the rehearsal dinner for before he leaves. Plus, I thought it would be fun for all of us to have an extended vacation together this week and next. Kind of like old times when we lived together." Her face lit up with the prospect.

"No, sorry, I can't. I'm only here for the day. Tomàs was called into work tonight, so I have to watch the kids." Desi grimaced. "It would have been fun though."

"Oh well, no worries. We'll have plenty of time to spend together before the wedding. Come in, come in." She motioned us through an imposing doorway.

Inside, the ceiling was open all the way to the second floor, creating a grand entry, complete with a wood and wrought iron chandelier.

"It's beautiful." I gazed up at the chandelier and then took in the contemporary artwork on the walls. "How long has your family owned the property? Were they the original owners?" I remembered hearing from Beth that the Lake

Elinor area had been a popular choice for summer homes in the early twentieth century.

Becca's eyes sparkled. "Yes, the property has been in my family since my grandparents bought it when they were first married. As you may have guessed, the house isn't original. My grandparents built a small cabin on the lake, but as our family grew larger they decided to tear it down and build something a little bit more accommodating for everyone." She beamed with pride as she surveyed the room. "I love it here and try to get over this way as much as possible with my work schedule."

"Well, it's gorgeous." I moved closer to a painting on the wall to inspect it. My dad had always wanted a lake house in Idaho, where we lived, but he and my mother were both teachers with limited incomes, and they had prioritized other things. Maybe now that he and my mom had separated, he'd use some of their savings to purchase a lake house.

"Thank you." She motioned for us to follow her to the rear of the house. "Everyone's out on the deck. It's such a beautiful afternoon."

We followed her out to a deck overlooking the lake, with the Chihuahua skittering along the hardwood floors behind us. The slow melodic tempos of a soft rock group wafted into the house when Becca opened the door to the deck. A group of five people sat on a comfortable patio set. Our arrival caught their attention.

"Desi." A woman with long wavy blonde hair popped up from the low-slung cushioned chair she had been sitting in. She wore figure-hugging jeans and a blouse that hadn't come from a rack at Target. Desi walked closer to her and they hugged.

"Hi, Lindsay. It's been awhile."

"It has," the woman said in a saccharine sweet tone. "How long has it been, anyway?"

"I think it's been since my wedding seven years ago." Desi looked around at the others on the deck. "I can't believe it's been that long since I've seen any of the old gang."

"You know, I think you're right." Lindsay turned to a man who was leaning against the railing. "You remember Declan, right?" There was a sharpness to her words, and her mouth twisted like she'd sucked on a lemon when she said the man's name.

"Of course." Desi gave Lindsay an odd look, as though she'd observed the same thing I had. "How is everything with you guys? Are you still living in Arwood?" She glanced between Declan and Lindsay. I noticed Becca cringe and I wondered what Desi had walked into.

"We're divorced," Declan said.

"Not quite yet. But hopefully soon," Lindsay said under her breath. Her soon-to-be ex shot her an icy death glare in return.

"Not soon enough."

"Declan plans to take all of our assets and jet away with one his bimbos."

He cringed. "Not quite, but definitely far away from you."

The venom dripping from their exchange silenced everyone else on the deck.

To change the conversation, Desi put her hand on my arm and said to the rest of the group, "This is my sister-in-law, Jill. She works at the Boathouse with my mom. Since my mom wasn't able to be here this weekend, Jill is going to be managing the wedding rehearsal and pre-wedding preparation."

All eyes were on me. I took a deep breath and smiled at them with as much confidence as I could muster. A tall man with dark curly hair rose from his chair and came over to shake my hand. His grip was firm and his smile pleasant. I had a feeling that he was one of the good guys.

"Nice to meet you," he said. "I'm Bill, Becca's fiancé. I'm glad you were able to make it out here. Becca and I are so excited to be having our wedding at the Boathouse. We both fell in love with it when we toured it last winter." He wrapped his arm around Becca and smiled jovially at us.

"Nice to meet you too." I smiled back at him. "It's great to meet so many of Desi's friends from college. I've heard a lot about all of you."

The last two people on the deck, a blond man of medium height and a woman with straight black hair, walked over to our group. He stretched out his hand.

"I'm Jared, one of Bill's partners at the dental office."

"And I'm Isabel, Becca's cousin." The dark-haired woman and I exchanged smiles.

Becca broke apart from her fiancé and addressed Desi and I. "I'm so sorry, girls, where are my manners? Would either of you like something to drink?"

The others had gone back to doing whatever they had been doing when we arrived. I noticed that Declan and Lindsay were standing as far apart on the deck as possible.

Desi responded first. "Sure, it's really hot today. I'd love a drink. What do you have?"

Becca laughed. "Oh, we have a little of everything. This whole vacation is our pre-wedding party. My last days as a single woman. C'mon. All the drinks are in the kitchen." She motioned for us to follow her. As she walked, she turned her head back to us and said, "We have margaritas and daiquiris, or wine and beer if you'd like that. I could even brew you a cup of Keurig coffee."

I wasn't sure about drinking alcohol on the job, so I asked Becca for a cup of coffee.

Desi looked at me and shrugged. "Well, I'm off the clock. I'll take you up on that margarita."

"I'm with you. I need something cold today." Becca smiled. "So, two frozen margaritas and a coffee?"

We nodded. We were alone in the kitchen, and Desi and I leaned against the counter while Becca prepared our beverages.

"What's going on with Declan and Lindsay? How long ago did they file for divorce?" Desi asked hesitantly.

Becca sighed. "About two months ago." She plucked a coffee mug from a cupboard and banged it on the counter next to the coffeemaker.

"Oh, no. I didn't realize that." Desi was quiet for a moment. "Were they separated for long before that? I know they've always bickered, but now there's so much animosity between them."

"A couple of months," Becca answered, inserting a pod into the machine and punching the brew button. "It should be finalized soon, thank goodness. They've been a nightmare to be around. When Bill and I asked them to be part of the wedding party, they were still together. We had no idea how stressful it would be to have them both around at the same time." She frowned. "They're some of our best friends and Declan is Bill's business partner, but still... this hasn't exactly been the fun week I'd anticipated." Her eyes filled with tears. "I'm a little worried they're going to ruin our wedding." She wiped her eyes with the back of her hand. "That sounds so awful and I feel bad for them, but I want everything to be perfect on our special day."

Desi put her arm around Becca. "Don't worry. I'm sure everything will be fine. What's the worst that can happen?"

Becca smiled tentatively. "I hope so."

The Keurig beeped and she removed my mug, setting it on the counter. She turned to me and said, "Oh! But don't forget to keep Declan and Lindsay separated at the rehearsal dinner. Don't let them sit anywhere near each other." She shuddered. "That would be a disaster."

I whipped out the small notepad I'd brought with me. Becca had sent us a seating chart a few months ago, and I wasn't sure who was sitting where. I made a note of her special request, then closed my notebook.

"Now," Becca said, gesturing to the refrigerator, "would you like some cream for your coffee?"

"No, black is fine. Thanks."

She handed me the cup of steaming black coffee.

"Thanks." I took the cup from her, blowing on the steamy surface.

She smiled at me, then turned to Desi. Her expression had turned mischievous. "Now for the good stuff. Do you want a strong margarita or an extra-strong margarita?"

"So many choices," Desi laughed. "I think I'll go with the extra-strong margarita. I'm not driving anywhere today."

"A girl after my own heart." Becca grinned and added several shots of tequila and cups of margarita mix into the glass blender, then followed it with a scoopful of ice cubes. She crushed the ice until it was a frothy concoction and poured it into two large margarita glasses rimmed with salt. She handed one of them to Desi and kept the other for herself.

"Yum." Desi delicately licked the coarse salt off the edge. "You've always known how to make the best drinks."

I sipped my coffee and leaned against the counter,

slightly envious of their icy beverages. Becca picked up her glass and said, "Stay here. I'm going to go out to the deck to ask everybody else if they'd like to have their drinks refreshed."

When we were alone in the kitchen, Desi and I exchanged glances.

"This is not going to be fun," she said.

"I know. I'm so glad that Beth is going to handle the actual wedding, but I feel a little bad about it. Having two members of the wedding party at each other's throats won't make it easy for her."

"I know, and it's so weird because they were the perfect couple in college and we all thought that they were the ones who were going to make it. Now look at them... you'd never know they had been best friends at one time."

"This house is gorgeous though." I admired the chef's kitchen, complete with a professional stove and yards and yards of marble countertops. "I wouldn't mind staying here. Are you sure you can't talk Tomàs into taking time off so you can stay out here and have a nice vacation? Maybe I could join you," I teased.

"It's even nicer than I remembered from when we came out here in college. I bet Becca or her parents have remodeled since then." Desi set her margarita glass on the counter and reached for the bowl of chips.

Becca came back in to prepare several drinks, and we helped her carry everyone's orders out to the deck.

"Thanks, honey," Bill said when she handed him a drink. He kissed the top of her head and she blushed. "Are you and Jill ready to discuss the wedding plans?"

"I am," Becca said, turning to Desi. "Desi, have you met my cousin Isabel before? She's a restaurant owner too. You'd probably have a lot to chat about."

"I think we met briefly a long time ago. I'd love to compare notes with her."

I left Desi chatting with Isabel near the deck railing and Becca, Bill, and I went into a study off the kitchen to go over their wedding plans.

2

"Now," Bill said. "I know we've talked with Beth about our wedding extensively, but there were a few things that we wanted to change." He and Becca sat across from me on a small love seat in the study.

I looked at him, trying to keep my eyes from bugging out. Their wedding was only a week away and, at this point, even a small change could put a wrench in things.

"What were you thinking about changing?" I got my notebook out and held my pen over it expectantly.

They looked at each other and Becca squirmed. "A few more relatives who I didn't previously know were attending are coming into town for the wedding. Do you think you might be able to add them on to the catering order?"

"How many is 'a few more relatives'?" I forced a smile, although I was pretty sure I didn't want to know the answer to my question.

"About thirty more?" She didn't sound too sure about it.

Bill nudged her shoulder with his. "Becca, I told you that we needed to find out earlier if they were coming or not."

She scrunched up her face. "I know, but my mom didn't

tell me that she'd invited all of our relatives in New York. I never thought to invite them since they live so far away. And I certainly never expected them to accept the invitation."

I consulted the catering list and made some quick calculations in my head. There was still time to get an additional order in with our supplier if I did it by tomorrow afternoon. I made a note to call the supplier. Frank wouldn't be happy with me, but he usually pulled through on my requests.

"That should be fine. We have a little wiggle room for the entreé order." Beth probably wouldn't be thrilled about it, but we generally wanted to do everything we could to accommodate clients, even those with last-minute changes. The Boathouse's business reputation was built on good customer service, and I didn't want to do anything to jeopardize its public image.

"There are a couple other things that I wanted to go over as well." Becca walked over to the desk and pulled out a giant binder from the drawer, bringing it back to where we sat. It was color-coded with at least twenty different tabs. She flipped to one of them, revealing a diagram of the seating arrangements in the Boathouse's main hall. She stabbed at one of the tables with her index finger.

"I have this one cousin who I don't want to be anywhere near my other cousin because they always get into fights, especially if there's alcohol involved."

Next to her, Bill rolled his eyes. I scribbled furiously on my own notepad as she opened another page in her binder.

"Also, we've decided that we want to have our Chihuahua, Tilly, walk down the aisle with our ring bearer and also be an additional ring bearer. Is there a place where we can keep her afterward while the reception is going on? My parents will be taking her home with them and watching her while we're on our honeymoon."

Although it might sound unusual to use a pet as a ring bearer, it was actually pretty common and I had dealt with this issue in the past. As I often brought Goldie with me to the Boathouse, I knew that we could set up one of the spare storage rooms for their dog and she'd be quite happy for a few hours.

"That'll be fine. We have somewhere for you to put Tilly while you're at the reception."

The tension evaporated from her shoulders and Bill wrapped his arm around her, squeezing her tight.

"Thanks so much, Jill. I'm glad we got a chance to talk with you about this. You'll make sure to let Beth know about our wishes for the wedding, right?" Some of Becca's stress had reappeared.

"Of course. I have everything in my notepad that we discussed, and I'll be sure to get it into the computer as soon as I get back to work tomorrow."

Bill turned to Becca and said, "See, I told you it would be just fine."

She blushed and leaned into him. "I know. But sometimes I tend to be a control freak and I wanted to make sure this will all be perfect."

I stood. "Don't worry about a thing. We do weddings all the time. Everything will be perfect for your special day."

Bill pushed himself up from the love seat and shook my hand. "Thanks so much. Will you be staying for the rest of the afternoon?"

I cast a glance out the French doors leading to the deck. Everyone out there was laughing and having a good time as the sun shone down on them and the glittering blue water below. I hadn't relaxed like that since my trip to Jamaica with Adam a couple of months ago. I had a minor flashback to how wonderful it had been to sit in the sun without a care in the world. But now I was back in the real world, and I had plenty of things to worry about.

"I don't know. I forgot to bring sunscreen and I burn easily. It's probably not a good idea."

"No problem," Becca said. "I've got sunscreen here you can use. It's all-organic. You'll love it."

"Oh." I couldn't think of any other reason why I couldn't stay. What did I absolutely have to get done today? I mentally reviewed everything on my to-do list. I needed to check over the catering orders for all of the next week's events, call a few clients back, and prepare a final invoice for an open-bar wedding we'd had last week. There was nothing that couldn't be put off for a few hours, and Adam and I had already planned for him to watch the kids this afternoon. After weighing my responsibilities, I smiled at him and said, "Sure, I can stay. That way Tomàs won't have to drive out here to pick up Desi before his shift at the police department, and she can still have a chance to visit with everyone."

"I'll be back in a minute," Becca said. She returned a few minutes later with a bottle of fancy sunscreen. After I slathered on a liberal amount of it on my pale skin, she linked her arm with mine and pushed open the French doors that led to the sun-filled deck.

Declan had left, but another man had taken his place. When he saw us, he introduced himself as Orson, a friend of Bill's from college.

"Nice to meet you. Are you staying here too?" I asked.

"I am. I couldn't say no to a vacation like this. I'm a software developer in San Francisco, so it's nice to get away from it all."

I nodded. "I'm sure." Desi beckoned to me from where

she stood near the railing. "Oh, my sister-in-law is calling me. It was nice to meet you."

He nodded, then went over to the seating arranged around a fire pit, and I made my way over to Desi. I noticed that Orson had sat down right next to Lindsay, and she was laughing and throwing her hair back in response to something he'd said. I didn't know what that was all about, but it wasn't my business.

"Hey. Bill invited me to stay for the rest of the day, so I was thinking I could drive you home later. Then Tomàs doesn't have to worry about it."

She smiled. "That would be great. Maybe we can even get a ride in Declan's boat."

"Boat?" I leaned over the railing and peered at the dock below. "Wow, that is a nice boat."

"Yes, apparently it's his pride and joy. I had to listen to him describing its attributes to me for way too long while you were in there with Becca and Bill."

On the boat, Declan was painstakingly cleaning each seat and seat cushion with a cloth and a bucket of water.

"Whoa. He does take that seriously. I'd be afraid to eat or drink on it."

"Me too. But I wouldn't mind a ride." She grinned impishly, fueled by that extra-strong margarita. "Let's go ask him."

I allowed myself to be dragged down to the dock.

"Hi," she said to Declan. "After all that build-up, I wanted to see your boat close-up."

He looked it over with pride. "Here it is. Do you want a ride?"

"Sure." Desi turned to me and winked. "That would be great."

My phone beeped to alert me that I had a new e-mail. I

held up my finger to Desi to signal her to wait. After all, I technically was supposed to be on duty at the Boathouse. However, when I saw who it was from, I turned my phone off. Anything from Nancy Davenport could wait. My nemesis at Mikey's preschool was probably trying to guilt me into making cookies for a bake sale or something. I wasn't going to let her disturb my rare moment of free time.

Desi shot me a questioning look and I gave her a thumbs-up.

"Ready?" Declan asked.

We both nodded and he moved the bucket of cleaning supplies to the dock to allow us to climb aboard. With a twist of his hand, he started the motor and we were off. We zoomed straight across the still lake and then he made a fast turn, sending water spurting into the sky. Our boat was the only watercraft on the lake, and Declan made full use of our freedom.

Desi's laugh rang out over the roaring motor. "This is fun," she shouted.

Declan grinned at us. "One more time around the lake?"

I looked at Desi and she nodded.

When we returned to the dock, I felt as if some of my cares had drifted away in the boat's wake. "Thanks so much," I said as we disembarked.

"Yes, that was awesome," Desi said.

"You're very welcome. I'm going to moor my boat at the Boathouse next week in preparation for the wedding. Bill and Becca will use it as their getaway boat when they leave for their honeymoon. If you see me around, maybe we can take it out on the Sound."

"That would be great. Well, thank you again. We'll let you get back to your maintenance." I moved toward the grassy lawn.

He picked up his cloth again and wiped a speck of algae off the side of the boat. "No problem."

Desi and I walked up the gentle slope, giggling like schoolgirls.

"That was so much fun," she said. "I haven't been out on a speedboat like that since we came out here in college.

"Me neither," I admitted. "But now I'm wondering if I can talk Adam into getting a boat." Lincoln had a small boat and used to take Adam and me out fishing once in a while, but to the best of my knowledge, neither Desi nor I had gone out on the water since our kids were born. Until now, I hadn't realized how much I missed it. I added swim lessons for the kids to my mental to-do list.

"Desi! Jill!" Becca shouted from the deck. "Come up here, we're starting a game of charades and we need more people."

When we reached the upstairs deck, we found Lindsay, Jared, and Orson were on one team, with Becca, Bill, and Isabel on the other.

"Desi, come join us," Becca said. "I want my matron of honor on my team."

Lindsay tensed up when she heard Becca call Desi her matron of honor and said something under her breath that I couldn't make out.

Desi trotted over to them and I sat down near Lindsay, who rolled her eyes.

"Three on a team was plenty," she grumbled.

I shifted closer to Jared. Orson was glued to Lindsay's side throughout the game, but she kept making excuses to get up and look over the railing at Declan on the docks.

When the game was over, we dispersed. Lindsay went in the house, complaining of a headache.

"Do we have more beer?" Jared asked.

Becca shook her head. "Sorry, I think we're out. I'll pick up more next time I go to the store. Unless someone wants to go now?" She glanced around at those of us who were left.

Jared shrugged. "Don't look at me; my car is in the shop. But I'll be happy to tag along if someone else wants to drive."

"I'm beginning to wonder if you actually have a car," Becca teased. "Maybe you just like to bum rides off everyone else."

He scowled at her. "Haha, very funny. The dealership is having trouble getting the part in that they need to fix it. It should be ready soon though." His eyes turned to the lake. "Don't worry about it. Next time you go to the store is fine." He sighed dramatically. "I'll have to make do with one of your famous margaritas."

"Excellent," Becca said. "I'll go make up a pitcher right now. Desi? Jill? Do you want one too?"

The sun was getting lower, and I'd promised Adam I'd be home at my usual time.

"Desi and I had better get going."

Desi nodded. "I've got to close up the café."

Becca's lips turned down. "Oh, ok. Well, I'm glad you were able to stay. I'll see you tomorrow at the rehearsal."

While Desi said goodbye to her other friends, I drifted away to gaze out at the water. The lake was still, although I knew it was breezy out on the water. Only our side of the lake had been developed. Across from us, tall trees grew thickly on the lakeside, almost to the water line. This was a far cry from my windowless office. With the sun shining down, I was glad I'd made the decision to stay, even if it meant I'd have to get some work done after the kids went to bed.

3

*B*y the time I arrived home, my eyes stung from Becca's sunscreen and were watering furiously. Priority one after checking on the kids was to wash my face so I could see without tears streaming down my face. Adam had been home with the kids all day, so I wasn't sure what the house would look like.

I prepared myself for the worst, but was pleasantly surprised to find Adam at the stove making dinner. Goldie bounded over to me to say hi, then retreated to his doggie bed, thumping his tail with happiness to have everyone home. Mikey was playing with his Legos in a corner of the living room, and Ella slept quietly in her swing. There weren't even any stray Cheerios on the floor. I set my notebook and purse on my desk in the living room and walked into the kitchen.

"Hi, honey. How was work?"

"It was fine. Desi and I went out to a client's place on Lake Elinor. An old friend of hers is getting married at the Boathouse, and she's the matron of honor." I dabbed my eyes with Kleenex. "It was a little stressful because two of her friends who are in the wedding party are getting a divorce and kept sniping at each other."

"Lake Elinor? Isn't that out by Morrow?" He seemed to finally notice me rubbing my eyes. "Hey, what's wrong with your eyes? Are you ok?"

"Oh, it's this sunscreen Desi's friend Becca gave me. I hadn't planned to stay at the lake long, but they convinced me to stay and play hooky from work. I don't know if I'm allergic to the sunscreen or if I just sweated too much at the lake." I stared at Adam, not surprised that my impaired vision made his face look blurry. "Would it be ok with you if I go take a shower?"

"Sure, I've got everything set for dinner. Mikey's been playing over there for hours." He gestured to the corner. "I planned on letting Ella sleep until dinnertime."

"Thanks. I'll try to hurry." I trudged up the stairs, surprised at how exhausted I felt after what hadn't been that tough of a work day. Being in the same place as a couple going through a nasty divorce had drained me. How two people who had once loved each other could now harbor such animosity toward each other was baffling.

Recently, Adam and I had made more of an effort to prioritize our marriage, and I hoped that divorce would never come up in our future. Then again, I'd never expected it to happen to my parents either. I pushed the negative thoughts out of my head and forced myself to live in the moment and enjoy my hot shower.

After a nice long shower, I emerged from the water with my eyes pleasantly clear and free of the stinging sensation that had sent me there in the first place.

I paused on the stair landing. No sounds came from the kitchen, and the only thing I heard from the living room was an odd ripping sound. Was Adam still cooking dinner?

I turned the corner and peered into the living room. I didn't see Adam, but what was Mikey playing with? My heart stopped and I prayed I was wrong. My gaze darted to the desk. The purse was still there, but the notebook I'd set next to it was missing. *Oh please, not my notebook.* Over by the fireplace, I heard the sound of paper being savagely torn. I rushed over to my son.

"What are you doing?" I screamed frantically. He stopped, staring up at me wide-eyed.

I grabbed the notebook from his hands and rifled through it. My worst fears had been realized. The notes that I had taken painstakingly at Becca's lake house were missing. I frantically scanned the pages on the floor and died a little when I saw the pieces that had been shredded by little four-year-old fingers. I closed my eyes and counted to ten. I'd already scared Mikey half to death by yelling at him, and there wasn't much I could do now.

But where had Adam been this whole time? Hadn't he noticed Mikey tearing paper instead of playing with his Legos? I turned to my son and put my finger under his chin to tip his head up until his eyes met mine.

"Honey, these were Mommy's good papers. Please don't ever touch anything on my desk, ok? It's really important."

Mikey's chin wobbled. "Sorry, Mommy. I won't do it again."

I gathered up all of the pages that I could. I certainly didn't want to tell Becca and Bill that I'd let my four-year-old destroy my record of all of the requests they'd made for their rehearsal dinner and wedding. I'd have to remember everything that I could and hope for the best. I consoled myself with the thought that there hadn't been too many major things, and I was sure I could piece most of it together from memory.

Just then, Adam walked in from the garage holding an armful of bags of frozen vegetables and meatballs. I held out the notebook to him, pages hanging haphazardly from the coiled wire spine.

"I thought you were going to watch him."

He looked from Mikey's guilty face over to me and then back again to Mikey. His face turned white. "I was watching him. I went into the garage to get some veggies for dinner, and I got distracted by cleaning out the freezer. I swear I was only gone for five minutes though." He peered at my face. "Was there something important in there?"

I sighed. "Yeah, kind of. It had all the information about what the client wanted for their rehearsal dinner tomorrow."

His lips turned downward. "I'm sorry, honey. I didn't think he would get into trouble that quickly. He's been sitting there playing Legos all day. I figured he would be there until I came back."

I thawed a little. It wasn't like I had eyes on Mikey 100 percent of the time when I was in charge either. Sometimes I had to get things done.

"It's ok. I'll figure it out."

"Is there anything I can do to help? Maybe piece together some of the scraps?"

I stared down at the notebook and the strips of paper in my hand. The edges were twisted unrecognizably. It would take a professional CSI unit to put it back together properly. I didn't have that kind of time. "I don't think so." I changed the subject. "How was everything today?"

He looked relieved. "The kids were good. I didn't get as much done on planning out my office as I'd hoped, but all in all, it was a pretty good day."

"Did you fill out the paperwork for the office lease?" I set the notebook down on the counter and perched on the edge of a barstool.

Brenda, one of my good friends who was a local real estate agent, was helping my husband find a space for his solo law practice. He'd cut down to part-time hours at his old firm and was now making progress on opening up his own office. When he'd been full-time, between work travel and long hours, the kids and I had barely seen him. I liked that he was now home more to help with the kids, but having him underfoot most of the time was taking some getting used to. I was happy I had my work at the Boathouse to get out of the house, and soon he would have his own business to occupy his time.

"I did. Brenda said she'll turn it in, and we should know something by Friday. She said to say hi to you."

"Good, I'm glad you were able to touch base with her. Is there anything I can do to help with dinner?" I scanned the kitchen. The sink was almost empty, and the counters were reasonably clean. Adam was turning into Super Dad.

He smiled. "I think I've got it under control." He stuck frozen green beans in the microwave and punched some buttons, then flipped on the burners of the gas stove to heat some water. "Why don't you go sit down at the table and see if you can repair some of the damage from our little tornado over there." He motioned to Mikey, who had now demolished his brick town and appeared to be pretending that a King Kong–like monster was taking over everything.

I grinned. "That sounds like a good plan." It was probably best to get everything down on paper before I forgot what the client had told me. Our cat, Fluffy, wound herself around my feet, wanting to be fed. I took care of her, then quickly jotted down everything I could think of—extra people (call supplier), dog as ring bearer, and separate the cousins at dinner. By the time Adam approached me ten minutes later, I felt confident that I'd remembered all of their requests and changes.

"You know, honey," he began, "we may need to think about finding a more permanent babysitting solution for the kids." He looked over at Mikey and Ella, who was still asleep in the bouncer. "Once I get my practice up and running, I'm not going to have much time to watch the kids during the day, and you've been really busy with your work."

He quickly added, "I'm very happy you've found something you enjoy, but we can't always depend on my mom to watch the kids because she has responsibilities at the Boathouse too."

I leaned back against the couch cushions. When I first started working at the Boathouse, Beth had told me that it would only be a part-time position. Well, during the busy summer season, part-time had turned out to be over forty hours per week. I knew my mother-in-law was happy to watch the kids when she was available, but Adam was right —she had her things to do.

"I know. I'll look into it." I felt a little twinge of guilt and worry at the thought of finding a non-family member to babysit my kids on a regular basis. We'd sent Mikey to the Busy Bees Preschool for two years now, but for some reason that seemed different than having a stranger in my house watching my children. Before having kids, I'd never given a second thought to how difficult it would be to find good childcare. I'd somehow assumed we'd easily find a good daycare and be able to happily drop them off every morning. No one had warned me about how complicated all the arrangements would be or how much it would affect me emotionally.

However, even with all of those considerations, I knew in

my heart that going back to work now was the right choice for me and my family. Without my income from the Boathouse, it would be financially difficult for Adam to strike out on his own. Having him leave his busy corporate law job would be better for our family in the long run. We just had to make it through the growing pains of our new roles.

Adam walked into the kitchen and busied himself at the stove, stirring the noodles and what I assumed was a pot of spaghetti sauce. The timer binged and he expertly drained the spaghetti noodles in a strainer in the sink. The aroma of tomato sauce and pasta filled the air, and I realized how hungry I was.

"Time for dinner," he called out. "Mikey, go wash your hands."

Mikey bounced up from the floor and ran into the bathroom and back again impossibly fast. "I'm starving, Daddy."

Ella banged her fists against her chubby thighs and babbled to tell us she was hungry too.

Adam looked over at me. "I did feed them lunch, I swear."

I laughed. Ella stared at us and I plucked her from her bouncer. "I'm going to go change her. Can you and Mikey set the table while I'm gone?" I left without waiting for a response.

When I came back downstairs, I found Adam serving up our dinner at a nicely set table while Mikey waited patiently in his chair, already wearing a bib to guard his shirt from the spaghetti sauce. It was a picture-perfect family scene. Maybe, just maybe, everything would work out well with our new careers. I crossed my fingers that that would be the case.

4

For Becca and Bill's rehearsal dinner, the Boathouse's staff had set up a long table in the main room and covered it with a navy blue tablecloth. The table was set with white linens and silver-trimmed dishes. With the sun starting to sink outside, we'd opened the barn doors to the deck to allow everyone to see what promised to be a gorgeous sunset. All that was left was for the attendees to arrive.

"It looks great, Jill," said a voice from behind me. I spun around. Desi had snuck up on me and was examining the setup. She was flying solo tonight, and Tomàs was home with the kids. I watched her assess the room, eager to hear what she thought of it. She'd managed many more events than me when she'd worked at the Boathouse.

"Do you really think it looks ok?"

She gave me a quick hug. "Of course. It looks great. Just as good or better than my mom could do it." She smiled at me.

I sighed with relief. This was one of the first events that Beth had given me to manage completely on my own, and I didn't want to mess it up, especially because it was for friends of Desi.

"Are we rehearsing first or after dinner?" Desi asked.

I looked at my watch. "Becca wanted to have the dinner first because we had to schedule the event so late to accommodate work schedules."

She nodded, then smiled and waved at someone behind me.

"This looks wonderful." Becca clapped her hands together and beamed. "Will the buffet table be in the same place for our wedding reception?"

I checked my notes. "Yes, it will be. Do you want it somewhere else? We have a few more options, but I thought with the large number of people you have, it would be better to have it off to the side."

"Works perfectly. Our head table will be up there though, right?" She motioned to a location on the raised platform. "I want to be able to see all of our guests."

"Of course." I jotted it down in the notebook.

"Oh, there are my parents. Thanks, Jill—I'm so excited to see what this will look like for our reception." She hurried off to meet an older couple at the door, escorting them to a place of importance near the head of the table.

I exited the room to check on the new arrivals in the lobby. The front door opened and Isabel came in, along with a man I assumed was her husband. She made the introduction and then said, "This is such a beautiful location. I can't believe I've never been in here before."

"Thank you. The other guests are right through there." I pointed at the main room. Isabel and her husband drifted away to examine the prints of historic Ericksville that hung on the lobby walls.

Another guest came in, and I repeated the directions.

Angry voices drifted in from the parking lot through the open door. Was something wrong? I ducked outside to check out the situation. When I saw who was making all the ruckus, I slid behind a post, out of sight.

Lindsay, Jared, and a couple of other people were standing in the parking lot next to a BMW that I recognized from the lake house. About ten feet away, near the sidewalk, Declan stood next to a slim woman with frizzy blonde hair. She wore Lycra pants, a tank top, and running shoes. At the moment, her face was flushed, not from jogging, but from the exertion of arguing with Declan. I couldn't hear what they were saying, but she was waving her arms around passionately. His face was as red as his polo shirt, but his expression was stony.

While I was at Lake Elinor, Lindsay had made some crack about him having tons of affairs and ruining their marriage. Was she one of Declan's extramarital affairs? The woman held up her hand dismissively and jogged away. He stood there for a moment, swigged from a flask he pulled from his pocket, and then joined the rest of the group. I slipped inside, hoping they hadn't seen me. For some reason, Lindsay wasn't fond of me, and I didn't want to give her anything else to complain about.

When all the guests arrived, they were seated according to name cards at each place setting, just the way Becca had wanted it. The catering staff took drink orders and staffed the buffet. I watched from the doorway as everyone chattered amongst themselves and ate happily. Everything was going according to schedule, and the actual rehearsal would start as soon as everyone was finished.

When most of the guests were finishing up their desserts, heated voices erupted from one end of the table. Suddenly, I knew what I had forgotten from the destroyed notebook. Icy dread spiraled up through my torso, numbing my brain.

In Becca's original seating chart, Lindsay and Declan were seated across from each other. But she had made that decision before she knew they were getting divorced. When I'd met with her at the house on Lake Elinor, she'd specifically requested that I seat them as far away as possible—a request that I'd noted and that had later been torn apart by the little but oh-so-destructive hands of a four-year-old before I could review my notes and commit it to memory.

Now Lindsay stood with a wine glass in her hand, shouting over the table at her soon-to-be ex-husband. Wine sloshed out of her glass as she punctuated each word with hand movements. The man closest to her leaned in toward the woman next to him to avoid being hit by flying crimson droplets.

Lindsay seemed to be berating him about some other woman, and I wondered if the woman from the parking lot had been the source of their separation. The catering staff huddled in the corner with their mouths agape. Everyone's eyes were fixed on the squabble. I caught the eye of our catering manager, Lizzie, and she surreptitiously cleared away the alcoholic drinks from that end of the table. Orson came over to Lindsay and put his hand on her arm, but she shrugged him off.

Becca and Bill exchanged glances, and she rose from her seat at the head of the table to approach their friends.

"Lindsay. Can you please come and help me with some of the props for our rehearsal? I need help from my bridesmaids," she said in a beguiling voice.

Lindsay glared at Declan. "Gladly. Anything to get away from this cheating jerk."

"It wasn't about that, and you know it." Declan threw his

napkin down on the table and pushed his chair away from the table. "But it doesn't matter anyway—I'm leaving." He stalked out of the room, weaving a little as he walked. Bill chased after him, but came back a minute later. Becca gave him a questioning look, but he just frowned and shook his head.

I glanced at Desi, but like most of the other guests, she wore an expression of shock over the spectacle she'd just watched. I walked up to the microphone.

"All right, everyone, I think now would be a good time to start the rehearsal."

Everyone got up, and the catering staff made short work of clearing the dishes and tables away to allow room for the rehearsal.

When all of the wedding party was in place, Bill said, "I need someone to fill in for Declan so we don't get the order of the groomsmen mixed up."

Becca scanned the room, her eyes landing on me. "Jill, can you take Declan's place tonight? That way, on our wedding day, you can tell him what he needs to do."

I didn't really want to be a groomsman for the night as I had a hundred things to do—monitor the staff, work on the table arrangements for their wedding, and check on the food supplies for the next week, among other things—but how could I say no? It was my fault that they were short a groomsman in the first place.

"Sure," I said. "I'd be happy to."

I kept a close watch on the door, but Declan never came back inside. Later, when all of the guests were gone and I'd locked up to go home myself, I noticed someone down on our floating docks. I moved closer to get a better look.

"Hey, Declan!" I called out from the deck as I walked toward him. "Are you ok?"

He was sitting cross-legged on the dock, surrounded by beer bottles.

"I'm fine," he said, slurring his words. He stood to prove his point but was so unstable that he almost fell over into the inky blackness of the water.

He was in no condition to be alone out there, and I could tell I wasn't getting home any time soon.

I held out my hand. "C'mon. I'll help you get up to the deck."

"Fine, I'll go, but I don't need any help."

I rolled my eyes. This wasn't the first time I'd had to escort an inebriated guest to a safer location. Usually it was because they were doing something stupid like trying to re-enact the scene in the movie *Titanic* by leaning out over the deck railing and pretending to fly.

When he was safely on the deck behind the railings, I went back down to collect the beer bottles before they fell into the water. In that short period of time, Declan disappeared. I hadn't heard any splashing, so I was fairly confident he hadn't pulled a Titanic.

I deposited the bottles in the trash receptacle and searched all of the outdoor areas on the Boathouse property, but there was no sign of him. My car was the only one in the parking lot, and I hoped he'd called someone to come pick him up because he was in no shape to drive.

5

After searching fruitlessly for Declan on the Boathouse property, I headed home. I unlocked the door and stepped into the house. Silence. The kids were asleep.

I dropped my keys on the entry hall table and entered the living room, sniffing the air. Something smelled good.

"Hey." Adam sat in the recliner, balancing his laptop on his legs, with Goldie at his feet. "There's lasagna left over from dinner. Do you want some?"

"No, I ate earlier. Thanks." I sighed dramatically and flopped onto the couch, pulling an afghan over me.

He raised an eyebrow. "Ok, what happened?"

I groaned and burrowed deeper into the pillows on the couch. Finally, I looked up at him. "Remember how I told you one of the bridesmaids and a groomsman were going through a nasty divorce?"

He nodded. "Did something happen between them?"

I closed my eyes, as if I could wish away the memories. "I sat them across from each other at the rehearsal dinner."

Adam gave me a strange look. "Why was that such a bad thing? Surely they're able to be civil to each other."

I groaned again. "Apparently not. They specifically requested not to sit next to each other, or rather, the bride had requested that they be seated as far apart as possible."

"And you forgot about this." He set his laptop on the coffee table and gave me his full attention. "Ouch."

I glared at him. "It was all in the notebook that Mikey tore up."

He had the good grace to flush. "Honey, I'm so sorry. I swear I was only gone for a couple of minutes when he did it."

"I know," I said. "I don't know how he gets into things so quickly. It's not your fault. Anyways, what's done is done." I threw myself backward into the couch cushions again.

"So what happened? Did they get in a huge fistfight? Was there blood spilled?" He laughed at his own words, then sobered when he caught my expression.

"Well, not a fistfight, but Declan and Lindsay pretty much ruined the night. Because the rehearsal dinner was later in the evening, we were planning on having the actual rehearsal take place after dinner. So when Declan stormed off, somebody had to fill in for him."

I shuddered, remembering how awkward it had been to take Declan's place at the rehearsal.

"It went fine, although I'm sure I wasn't as good a groomsman as Declan would have been. I'm now responsible for showing him what he needs to do at the real wedding. And if he's not in the right place at the wedding on Saturday, the bride isn't going to forgive me. I just hope he shows up for the wedding. He disappeared on me after I found him drunk down on the floating docks. I don't know how someone who could barely walk could get away so fast."

Adam stifled a laugh. "He probably called someone to pick him up. I'm sure he'll be there for the wedding." He tilted his head. "Somehow, I can't picture you as a groomsman."

I grimaced. "Yeah, well, there are pictures to prove it. Becca hired a photographer to be there for the rehearsal. I'm sure she got a whole camera full of photos of Declan and Lindsay duking it out over the dinner table."

He came over and sat down next to me, gently rubbing my back. "I'm sure it will be fine."

My eyes met his. "I know, but your mom usually helps me with events, I feel a little lost without her. Thank goodness she'll be here for the wedding."

As if on cue, Adam's cell phone rang. I looked at my watch. It was after ten o'clock. His work didn't usually call this late, especially now that he was wrapping things up at the law firm.

He held up the phone to check the caller ID, then pressed Incoming Call. "What's up, Dad? Is everything ok?" His face filled with concern. "Is she ok?" His father said something on the phone and Adam nodded. "Yes, I understand."

Had something happened to Beth? She had seemed so healthy when she left to go visit her sister in Portland, but I knew she had some health concerns.

I tugged on Adam's sleeve. "What's wrong?" I whispered.

He covered the mouthpiece on the phone. "Mom had some sort of heart palpitations while they were at the restaurant. She'll be fine, but they may have to do a minor operation. At the very least, they're going to have to stay in Portland for a while until she's well enough to travel."

He returned to the conversation with his father. I leaned back against the couch, stunned by Adam's news. I knew Beth had experienced some issues with her heart recently, but she'd assured me it wasn't serious. Something occurred to me. I tapped on Adam's shoulder and he looked up.

"When are they coming home?" I asked, my stomach filling with dread.

"I think in a couple of days." His dad said something, pulling Adam's attention back to the phone.

A couple of days? Bill and Becca's wedding was in a week. I breathed a sigh of relief. Beth should be back in time for the wedding. I did have some questions for her though about some other events.

"Can you ask if I can talk to your mom?"

He relayed my request to his father and then handed me the phone.

"Hi, Jill." Beth's voice sounded weaker than usual.

"Hi." I immediately felt bad for my selfish concerns about her missing the wedding. "How are you doing?"

She laughed. "I've been better. I thought we'd be on our way home tomorrow, but now I'm stuck in a hospital bed."

"Are you ok? Adam said you were having chest pain and palpitations."

"I was." She was quiet for a moment. "They want to put a stent in tomorrow."

"Oh." My mind raced.

"It's not a major operation, don't worry. I should be fine after it."

"Ok." I wanted to ask her questions about the upcoming Boathouse events and find out when she was coming back, but this didn't seem like the right time to do so.

On the other end of the line, Beth was quiet and someone was talking to her in the background.

"Hey, Jill, I've got to go. I'll call you tomorrow after the surgery."

"I love you, Beth."

"Love you too, honey."

With a lump in my throat, I handed the phone back to Adam and reached down to pet Goldie's silky ears.

When he finally got off the phone with his dad, he picked up his laptop and went back to work on it like nothing had happened. I stared at him, my mouth agape.

"Adam. Did your dad say how your mom was doing? She didn't sound great on the phone. Is the surgery really as minor as she said?"

He clicked on the trackpad then gave me a questioning look. "What do you mean? She's having surgery tomorrow. Dad says it's no big deal, and she seems in good spirits. The doctor said she's young and will heal quickly. The doctor there wants to recheck her in ten days though, so they're going to stay in Portland in case there are any complications."

"Ten days? I thought you said a couple of days." She'd miss the wedding. If my mother-in-law wasn't around, that meant responsibility for the wedding fell on me. I wasn't sure how Becca was going to react to the news that I'd be coordinating the biggest day of her life after I'd messed up the seating at her rehearsal dinner. I'd have to figure out a way to convince her that I could handle it.

"Yeah, I thought they'd be there for less time, but after you talked to Mom, Dad said it would be ten days." He tapped a few things on his computer, shut the lid, and regarded me thoughtfully. "I guess we'll have to find a babysitter for the kids sooner rather than later, huh?"

I rolled my eyes. "Yeah. That's on my to-do list as well." With Beth out of commission for a few weeks, if not months,

I needed to find somebody immediately who had full-time availability. I gave Goldie a final pat, then put my hand on Adam's arm and stood.

"I'm going to take my laptop out to the deck and work for a while, ok?"

He nodded. I got my computer off the desk in the living room, poured myself a glass of Chardonnay, and went out on the deck. The night air was crisp, a welcome change from the heat earlier in the day. I sat on a cushioned patio chair and propped my feet up on one of the small matching ottomans. Tapping my fingers on the laptop lid and gazing out at the twinkling lights of Willowby Island, I tried to unscramble all the thoughts that were mixing in my brain. After a few minutes, I gave up. I relaxed on the deck, enjoying the stillness of the night and sipping my wine.

When I came back inside the house, I found Adam on the couch, sound asleep, with his laptop resting on the edge of the coffee table. Goldie lay on the rug below him and thumped his tail when I approached his master. Adam looked so peaceful sleeping there that I closed his laptop, covered him with a blanket, and turned out the living room lights. Fluffy meowed at me to feed her and I acquiesced, then poured myself a half glass of wine, sipping it as I tiptoed upstairs.

I peeked at the kids in their rooms. Mikey and Ella were also sleeping soundly. After finishing my wine and getting ready for bed, I tried to fall asleep. Unfortunately, dreamland didn't come as easily to me as it had for the rest of my family. Thoughts of Declan and Lindsay fighting filled my mind, making it difficult to nod off. When I finally did, I had a nightmare that the minister hadn't shown up and the wedding had to be rescheduled.

6

To make sure everything was on track with the wedding, I woke up earlier than usual. The banging around downstairs told me that Adam was already in the kitchen, probably making coffee. When I joined him in the kitchen, the clock on the microwave read 6:30 a.m. Although I hadn't slept well, I was surprisingly refreshed and ready to take on the day.

"How was the couch?" I asked him.

He rubbed his neck. "Not the most comfortable place to sleep. I only meant to close my eyes for a few minutes, but I must have drifted off. Sorry, honey. But at least I finished the client e-mail I needed to send out last night."

He poured a cup of coffee and handed it to me. "Did you work out all the details for the big wedding?"

I frowned. "I tried, but my brain was fried." I glanced at the time on the microwave again. If I got over to the Boathouse now, I'd have at least an hour or two before anybody else showed up. Uninterrupted time to work would do a lot toward easing my nerves.

My eyes met Adam's. "Would you mind if I left early for work?"

He shrugged. "No, that's fine. I can take Mikey to school." He motioned to the toaster. "Do you want something to eat before you leave?"

I thought about it. Desi's shop, the BeansTalk Café, wouldn't be open this early in the morning, and I didn't think the espresso cart by the ferry dock had much in the way of food.

"Do we have any of those raisin bran muffins left?" I walked over toward the counter where I'd last seen them.

"We had raisin bran muffins?"

I laughed. "Yeah, I bought them at the store earlier this week. Mikey loves them." I rifled through the breadbox and found two muffins, one a pile of crumbles and one that was miraculously intact. I nabbed it and poured myself another cup of coffee— this time in a to-go container.

"This will do." I gave him a peck on the cheek and rushed out the door. I didn't have anywhere to go after work, and the weatherman had promised a gorgeous August day, so I opted to leave my minivan in the garage and walk the mile down to the Boathouse. I figured that the crisp morning air and exercise would help me clear my head before what would most likely be a busy day.

By the time I was a few blocks away from my house, I knew I'd been right. Walking to work was the perfect way to start my day. Puget Sound was calm, with nary a whitecap in sight. The water was dotted with boats carrying eager fisherman to their lucky fishing spots. Further out, the heavily wooded shores of Willowby Island silhouetted the green and white outline of the Ericksville ferry.

I took in the view, ever grateful to live in the Northwest. I inhaled with a deep breath, allowing the salt-tinged air to fill my lungs. Seagulls flew overhead, dipping down into the water as they spotted breakfast. These were the kinds of days that made us all want to live in the Pacific Northwest and completely forget about the months and months of rain that we endured every winter.

When I reached the foot of the hill on Ferry Street, I turned left toward the Boathouse. I passed by the BeansTalk Café, but the lights were out. Desi wasn't due to open for another hour. A few joggers passed over the lighthouse grounds in between the café and the Boathouse, but they just smiled at me and jogged past without a word. The parking lot at the event center was empty, and I congratulated myself on my good fortune to be able to work uninterrupted for a few hours. To my surprise, when I opened the door, the smell of baking pastries filled the air. It wasn't Desi's day to bake, and I hadn't seen her car in the parking lot. Usually, Beth would be here on a Friday. But Beth wasn't in town, I remembered. I assumed my in-laws had called Desi last night as well.

I walked toward the kitchen, and Desi popped her head out into the hallway.

"Hey," she said, "I wondered when you'd get here. I hoped I'd have a chance to see you this morning."

"I decided to come in a little bit early today to get things done for Becca and Bill's wedding."

A timer beeped from inside the kitchen, and she gestured for me to come in. She pulled éclair shells out of the oven and laid them on a rack to cool. With a deft hand, she piped vanilla custard into the centers of a cooled batch of pastries.

"I take it my mom called you and Adam last night too?"

She set the empty pipette on the counter and scooped more custard to refill the tool.

"Actually, your dad called us. I think the doctor was in talking to your mom. How do you feel about it?"

"It wasn't the best news, but I know Mom is basically healthy." She peered at me. "Do you need any help with Becca and Bill's wedding? I know my mom is usually around to manage big events."

I didn't say anything at first. Did Desi think I wouldn't be able to handle it? I checked her expression. No, she didn't look overly concerned. I took a calming breath.

"I think I have everything under control at the moment, but I'll let you know if I need help. Thanks."

She shrugged. "No problem. If you need anything, just let me know. I'm already involved with the wedding, so I'm happy to help out wherever you need me." She handed me a plate with a chocolate-iced éclair on it. My mouth instantly started watering when the plate touched my hand. With the other hand, I jiggled my to-go container of coffee. It was empty save a few drops in the bottom. I stared at it sadly.

She grinned and pointed at the back counter. "There's fresh coffee in the pot. I made it about an hour ago."

I smiled at her gratefully. Somehow my sister-in-law could always read my mind when it came to food and drink.

"Do you mind if I take this to go?" I needed to get cracking on my work if I wanted to take advantage of this time to myself.

She waved her hand in the air. "Of course not. I've got to get over to the café pretty soon anyways, so I need to finish these."

I slung my bag over my shoulder and walked to the other side of the building, clutching the plate and the cup of coffee. In my office, I docked my computer and turned it on, my fingers bouncing on the keys, ready to type out my to-do list.

I had a few options when it came to the wedding. I could ask Desi for help, but she already had a lot going on, and she was in the wedding party. I was sure she'd been sincere in her offer to help, but I didn't want to depend on it or spoil her experience as a bridesmaid. I took a deep breath. Everything was going to be fine. I'd managed several weddings before with Beth's guidance, and I knew that I could handle everything. However, the debacle of a rehearsal dinner was throwing me a bit.

I opened the computer and listed the things that I needed to do for Becca and Bill's wedding. I wasn't sure if I'd be able to touch base with Beth anytime soon as she'd be undergoing surgery today, and I wanted to make sure that I wasn't missing anything.

After completing a lengthy list, I stared at it, then bit into the éclair, hoping that the rush of sugar and infusion of caffeine would help me decide what to do first. It did work for a while, and I completed a few quick tasks. When only more complicated projects remained, I stared at the computer screen again. In my previous career as a marketing manager, I'd only had to manage one client at a time. Now I was responsible for coordinating the intricacies of many events at the same time. Being a mom had prepared me for multi-tasking, but the list still overwhelmed me to the point of indecision.

Finally, I pushed myself up from the desk and walked down the hallway toward the deck. The fresh air had done wonders for me earlier, and I hoped it would do the same now. I could hear noise from the kitchen, so Desi was still in there. I didn't see anyone else.

I pushed open the double doors to the deck and the boat

dock. The exterior doors of the main event space were closed up tight, but the gate to the ramp for the boat dock swung on its hinges in the breeze. I closed the gate and paused for a moment at the top of the ramp.

Last night, the Boathouse's docks had been empty. Sometime since then, someone had tied up a shiny new boat at the middle slip. Although there was a red cover over most of the boat, I recognized it immediately as Declan's Bayliner Runabout. But what was it doing here?

I remembered Declan telling us that he had permission to dock it at the Boathouse for the week leading up to the wedding. The rehearsal dinner hadn't ended terribly late, but it still seemed odd that he would have taken his boat out on the Sound at night instead of waiting for morning light. I wasn't even sure it was legal to use the boat ramp after dark. But who was I to judge? Maybe it was what worked best in the wedding schedule. Beth's files had noted that Bill and Becca planned to leave their wedding in the boat and jet off to a romantic honeymoon on a cabin on Willowby Island.

The boat bobbed up and down in the water, and I decided to check it out further. When I met with Becca at Lake Elinor, Declan had given Desi and me a ride in his boat, but I hadn't had much time to admire it. Although I wasn't an expert on watercraft, like most people in the area I'd had my fair share of boating experiences out on the Sound and the neighboring lakes.

I ran my hands over the smooth fiberglass side of the Runabout. If I had a friend with a boat like this, I'd be begging them for rides all the time. There was nothing better than being out on the water on a beautiful sunny Pacific Northwest day. Lincoln owned a small fishing boat, but it was nothing compared to this one, which I estimated held about five to seven people at a time. Adam's family was more into a quiet day out fishing on the Sound than water-skiing on a lake, but there had been something exhilarating about racing across the water when Desi and I had gone out with Declan on his boat.

Out of the corner of my eye, I saw a flash of red under the surface of the water, similar in color to the covering on the boat. Something was caught on the portion of the mooring rope that dangled in the water. Had part of the cover fallen off?

I knelt on the rough wooden boards to get a closer look. The boat shifted away from the dock, and I realized that the object floating under the blue-green water wasn't part of the cover. A chill shot up my spine. A man's body was tangled up in the rope.

I screamed loudly and pushed myself back from the edge. I stumbled backward, falling to the dock with my hands sprawled to the sides. I sat up, pulling my knees up to my chest.

How could this be happening again? This wasn't the first dead person I'd found in the last few months. My gaze turned uncontrollably to the cliffs above the beach where I'd discovered the body of my deceased neighbor last spring.

"Jill, was that you screaming?" Desi burst out of the main building of the boathouse. "Are you ok?"

"I'm down here," I called out to her. She appeared at the top of the ramp to the dock.

"What are you doing down there?"

I couldn't get the words out. She pushed the gate aside and walked down the ramp toward me.

"Isn't Declan's boat gorgeous? I can see why he's so proud of it, although I'm going to scream if I ever have to hear him bragging about it again." She shook her head. "I'm not sure when he brought it over, but it was probably on

Becca's schedule." She paused and looked at me as if just now seeing the terror on my face. "What's wrong?" She scanned the dock.

I pointed into the water near the back of the boat. Her eyes followed my fingertip.

"Yeah, it's Declan's boat. I know."

"No," I said. "Look in the water."

Desi moved closer to the edge of the dock and her eyes widened. "Is that what I think it is?"

She stared at the red object in the water and then back at me.

"Unfortunately, I think it is."

"Who is it?" She backed away.

"I don't know."

Feeling a little more composed now, I stood and walked over to stand next to her. We both stared into the water. The body bobbed just below the surface of Puget Sound. A massive cruise ship went by, and even though we were protected by the jetty surrounding the Ericksville Marina, the waves shifted the boat a little away from the dock. The body rolled in the water, coming to rest face up in the water, then flipping back over as another wave came through.

Desi's face blanched. "Is that—"

I interrupted her. "Declan Becker."

We looked at each other.

"How did he get in the water?" I couldn't take my eyes off of the body.

She seemed to have the same problem. "Do you think he fell in last night? He had a lot to drink—maybe he never left. Did you see him out here when you locked up?"

"No, he was down here, but he was so drunk that I chased him off the docks and onto the deck. I came down here to clean up his beer bottles, but when I got back up to the deck, he was gone." Had he fallen off the deck? I peered up at the deck railings. No, they were too high to fall over accidentally, and I was sure that I would have heard something if he had fallen while I'd been here.

"Maybe he came back after I left?" My words were dull, and I felt like someone had stuffed cotton into my head. The gate from the Boathouse's deck to the parking lot was locked from the outside, but anyone who tied up at the dock could get out.

She chewed on her lip. "But if he was already here, where did his boat come from? I don't think you'd be able drive a truck and boat trailer from Lake Elinor all the way here, launch the boat, and tie it up to the dock if you were so drunk that you could fall into the water."

I shrugged. "I don't know. The boat definitely wasn't here last night. I would have seen it." I turned slowly around on the dock, checking to see if anything else was different. A few beer bottles lay on their sides behind a dock cleat.

I put my hand on her shoulder and pointed at the bottles. "I don't think those were there last night, but I might have missed them in the dark."

She eyed the beer bottles. "We'd better call the police."

"They're going to start thinking that I'm a magnet for dead bodies." This was the third one I'd found in less than a year.

"Jill," Desi said. "I mean this in the nicest possible way, but you do seem to have a way of finding bodies. I don't think I've ever met anybody else who has even found one, much less three.

I glared at her. "Just call the police."

She nodded and pulled out her phone. When the operator came on, she gave them the necessary information and hung up. Less than ten minutes later, sirens sounded in the parking lot.

"I'll go open the door to the Boathouse for them," she said. "You wait here."

"I can..." I started to squeak out, but she was gone. I sat back down again with my back to the boat, trying to avoid looking at Declan's body. The slapping of the water against the boat and the dock made me want to go over there, but I knew I didn't need to increase the chance of the horrifying image imprinting on my brain.

A crowd of people appeared on the deck in front of the Boathouse, with Desi in the lead. Emergency personnel hurried down the ramp toward Declan's Runabout. Their weight caused the floating dock to lurch up and down, and I almost lost my balance. I stared at the chilly water. I didn't want to end up in the drink like Declan had. I gave the police my information and, to lessen the load on the dock, I went up to the main deck where Desi watched the commotion from a position near the railing.

"We should call my parents and let them know about this," she said, her eyes locked on the recovery efforts down below. "I can't believe he's gone."

In the confusion over finding the body, I hadn't thought about Desi's friendship with Declan.

I touched her arm. "I'm so sorry. Are you ok? I know you've been friends for a long time."

She gave me a teary smile. "We were friends way back when, but not so much now. I just feel so bad for Lindsay. It's such a shock. At least she's at the lake house, so she'll have friends around when they notify her."

I stared at her. "Becca and Bill's wedding. Do you think they'll want to cancel it? I mean, Declan was a groomsman."

"I don't know. It's certainly a possibility."

We gazed down toward the dock where they were busy recovering Declan's body. A policeman walked up the ramp and approached us.

"Mrs. Andrews?" he asked, his eyes shifting between the two of us.

I held my hand up like a little kid. "I'm Jill Andrews."

He smiled at me disarmingly. "I have a few questions to ask you."

"Of course."

"You said you'd seen Declan Becker on the docks last night after the event."

I nodded.

"Had he been drinking at the event? Was he drinking on your dock?"

"Yes, but we didn't overserve him," I said quickly. "We cut him off after a few drinks, but I saw him with a flask earlier in the evening. When I saw him later, I managed to get him safely off the docks and to the upper deck. Then he just disappeared. I didn't see him again... I mean until I found his body this morning."

"We found some beer bottles on the dock near his boat. Do you think he came back with the boat and had a few beers out there?" He jutted his head toward the dock below.

"I'm sorry, I really don't know. His boat wasn't there when I left last night." Icy fear shot through me. Would the Boathouse be held liable for Declan's drinking?

He wrote something down on his notepad.

"We'll be in touch if we have more questions." He pivoted and returned to the rest of his team.

I knew I hadn't seen Declan out on the docks when I left the night before. His boat definitely hadn't been there. The most likely scenario was that he'd sobered up and returned with his boat, then had some celebratory beers and fallen off the dock, becoming entangled in his mooring lines.

Whatever had happened, it wouldn't be good publicity for the Boathouse.

I turned to Desi. "We definitely need to call your mom and dad. Do you think that Lindsay will sue?"

She scrunched up her face. "Sue? Why would she sue? Declan was probably drunk as a skunk." She flushed. "I shouldn't be talking ill of the dead. We don't know what happened."

"This is private property. If they determine we were negligent in some way, the Boathouse could be liable."

She sucked in her breath. "Do you really think that could happen?"

I stared blankly at the emergency personnel. "I really hope not." Having met Lindsay, though, I didn't think we'd have a chance of making it through this unscathed.

Desi slowly pulled her cell phone out of her pocket and speed-dialed her father. I watched her talk to him, much as I'd done yesterday with Adam.

She nodded a few times and paced around the deck in a circular pattern. "Ok, so you'll take care of calling the insurance company. Jill and I will figure out what we want to tell the press."

I gawked at her. The press?

She hung up and looked at me. "We need to come up with something to tell the news crews when they arrive."

I groaned. I did not want to deal with news crews.

"Ok. What should we tell them?"

"I think just stick with the basic facts. He was a guest at an event here last night, but we don't know what happened to him. The police can fill in the rest."

I nodded—that seemed easy enough.

She patted me on the shoulder. "Don't worry, it will be ok. No one is going to blame us for Declan's death. My dad said there was nothing we could've done to change what happened."

I hoped she was right.

7

*A*fter the police questioned us, Desi gathered up the pastries she'd baked that morning and left to go open the BeansTalk Café for the day. Even with all the commotion outside and the staff members trickling in to work the day's events, I felt strangely alone in the Boathouse. I admit I was a little shell-shocked by what had happened. Never in my life had I expected to see Declan's body floating under the water, tangled in a rope from his own boat. I pulled Lizzie aside to explain what had happened and instructed her to tell the rest of the staff as needed. We didn't have any events scheduled until that evening, and I fervently hoped things would be back to normal by then.

Although Lincoln had said there was nothing I could've done to change what had happened, I still worried about any potential lawsuits or negative publicity as a result of Declan's death on our property. I paused by the window in the main hallway that overlooked the docks. Outside, the police were still examining his boat and the adjacent boat dock. Reporters stood outside the Boathouse, talking into microphones. Overhead, the KINO news helicopter hovered over the water near the event center. I thought I even saw a news boat out in the water taking photos. It was all too much.

I ducked back into the Boathouse and scurried down the hall to my office. Sitting down at my desk, I buried my head in my hands. I had to get some work done. With Beth gone, there was way too much to do for me to slack off. I turned on my computer and checked my e-mail. The message from Nancy Davenport was still there, unread. I quickly scanned it and sighed. She had wanted me to come in by the end of this week to check in with her—I wasn't sure what for. It was already Thursday and I was probably in deep gerbil droppings for not getting in touch with her sooner.

The whirring of helicopter blades circling the Boathouse drew my eyes toward the windowless walls of my office. Part of me wanted to know what was going on outside, and the other part wanted to forget the whole morning had ever happened. I forced my attention back to the computer screen, but my eyes glazed over after less than a minute as I read the same three lines over and over again. I wasn't going to get anything done at the moment, so time to find out what Nancy wanted from me.

I avoided the few reporters who were still lingering outside the Boathouse and hiked up the hill, past the long-term ferry parking lot, to Mikey's preschool. Unlike this morning, the walk did nothing to soothe my nerves. I walked there as if in a daze, somehow avoiding any traffic as I crossed streets.

Outside of the school, in the parking lot, I spotted a minivan with a family of stick figures stuck to the back window—Nancy's car. I took a deep breath. Part of me had hoped that she wouldn't be there so I could get out of whatever it was that she wanted to talk to me about. Unfortunately, it looked like I wasn't going to get off that easily. I walked past the parking lot, stopping just short of the door to the Busy Bees Preschool and peeked in the side window.

Mikey was in there with the rest of his preschool class, sitting on the alphabet rug and listening to his teacher read them a story. A smile flickered across my lips. I loved seeing him so into a book, but I didn't want him to see me. As every mom knows, if you show up at your child's preschool in the middle of the day, just like the mouse and the cookie story, they're going to think it's time to come home. How was I going to avoid Mikey seeing me? Behind me, a car honked loudly at another vehicle.

I groaned. I could feel twenty sets of four-year-old eyes on me. Reluctantly, I pushed open the door, hoping that by some stroke of good fortune he hadn't seen me. Luck wasn't on my side. By the time the door slammed shut behind me, Mikey was in the lobby, bouncing around me.

"Mommy, Mommy!" he said. "Is it time to go home?"

I ruffled his hair. "Not yet, sweetie. I came in to talk to Mrs. Davenport, but then I have to go back to work. Remember, Grandma is in Portland, so I have to do some of the things she'd usually do at the Boathouse."

His face fell. We hadn't told him that Beth had been ill, just that she was staying longer with her sister. Still, he was used to seeing her almost every day, and he knew things weren't quite right in his world. I knelt to talk with him on his level.

"How about you and Daddy and Ella and I have a special dinner out tonight?"

"Really?" His face lit up.

I nodded solemnly. "Really."

"Where are we going?" He returned to bouncing enthusiastically in front of me.

"I don't know," I said mysteriously. "I was thinking maybe somewhere with pizza."

He bounced faster. "Pizza Palace? Where they have all the games?"

I held him in place and kissed his head. "Yep, that place."

The assistant teacher stood in the entrance to the classrooms.

"Sorry, Jill, he ran out before I could catch him." She beckoned to Mikey. "The rest of the class is still listening to Ms. Shana read a story." She held out her hand to him.

"Bye, Mommy," he shouted. "I want three pieces of pizza tonight, ok?"

"Sure, sweetie." I grinned as he ran off, following his teacher back to the classroom. Mikey's eyes were often bigger than his stomach.

I ducked my head into the office to see if Nancy was in there working on some paperwork. She was sitting at the computer with her back to me. I rapped sharply a few times on the office door and she turned, pulling her lips into what passed for a smile.

"Jill, nice to see you. I thought you weren't going to show up."

I smiled weakly at her. This was why I hated coming to my son's school unless I was there to pick him up and run. Nancy was so aggravating.

"Yes, of course," I said. "Work has been pretty crazy this week, and I just now had the chance to read your e-mail. What did you need to see me about?"

She gave me a look of disapproval, as if I'd committed

the sin of the century by not leaping at the chance to read an e-mail from her.

"I was e-mailing you about your parent volunteer commitment. Mikey is so excited about you being in his classroom next week." She shuffled some papers on the desk.

I had no clue what she was talking about. Being in his classroom? I didn't have any plans to be at the preschool next week. I narrowed my eyes at her.

"I'm not sure what you mean."

She shot me a condescending look. "Don't you remember? You signed up at the beginning of summer to be a parent assistant for next week's summer camp."

My blood ran cold. I vaguely remembered signing up to help out in my son's classroom sometime that summer. Summer was winding down, and I guessed that time was now. It wasn't that I didn't want to help out in his classroom, but this was not the right time to do it. Twisting threads of anxiety shot up through my chest, and I felt as if I couldn't breathe. I wasn't sure how I was going to manage Beth's responsibilities until she got back in addition to my own. This could put me over the top. I crossed my fingers behind my back.

"Is there anyone else who can do it? This is a really bad time for me. I could help out next month."

Her eyes bored into me, and she pursed her lips. "Jill, all of the parents have taken a turn helping out with summer camp. Do you really want to disappoint Mikey?"

I felt like a deer in the headlights, waiting for her to run me over. "It's not that I don't want to, it's just that there's so much going on right now at work."

She shook her head. "You know, Jill, we all have lives too. But this is for the kids."

I wasn't getting out of this one.

"Ok," I said reluctantly. "What do I need to do?"

She shoved a piece of paper at me. I read the details on it.

"I need to be here for the whole week? And for all four hours of summer camp?"

She sighed. "Yes, Jill, that is what you signed up for."

I took a deep calming breath to avoid passing out in the office from stress. With tight lips, I said, "See you next week."

As I walked back toward the front door of the preschool, I passed by the two gerbils racing around the wheel in their cage. I felt like that, as though I was a gerbil running around on a wheel. It wasn't supposed to be like this. I've given up my high-powered corporate job when I had Mikey, and only recently had returned to work. I thought working for the family business would allow me time to spend with my kids and give me the adult interaction that I desperately needed. *It's only temporary*, I told myself. I pushed open the door to the street outside and felt a sense of freedom as soon as I was out of eyesight of Nancy Davenport.

8

When I woke up on Friday morning, I felt much more relaxed and happy than I had the day before. As I'd promised Mikey, we'd all gone to the Pizza Palace for dinner. Surprisingly, Mikey had eaten three pieces of pepperoni pizza. My little boy was growing up so fast. Even Ella enjoyed it, although she was somewhat afraid of the giant dancing mice, which I couldn't blame her for. I tried to avoid them myself, even though as an adult, I knew they weren't real. Most of all, it was nice to have Adam home. I was hopeful that him having his own practice in Ericksville would be the best thing for our family.

My good mood dissipated when I pulled into the Boathouse's parking lot. A horde of reporters was camped out near the door. As soon as they saw me, they rushed over in a teeming mass of microphones and video cameras. They bombarded me with questions about Declan's death, each talking over the other.

Their incessant questions buzzed around me like bees swarming from a hive. I stood still for a second, trying to make sense of it all. Why were there so many reporters here? I knew it was a small town, but we'd found Declan's body the day before, and it wasn't like there was the notoriety of murder associated with his death. While tragic, it was clearly an accident.

I pushed through the crowd to reach the front door, not giving them any statements. Before I could unlock it, I felt a hand on my arm. I turned, and regarded the owner of said arm with distaste. It was Niely MacDonald from the *Ericksville Times*. Our past interactions hadn't been pleasant, but I had to give it to her, she had guts. She'd managed to shove her way to the front of the crowd, getting to me ahead of all of the Seattle reporters.

"Mrs. Andrews," she said. "Do you have anything to tell me about the murder of Declan Becker?"

"No comment," I said as I fought with the lock. It finally gave, and I opened the door then hesitated. Had she just said murder? I narrowed my eyes at her.

"What do you mean murder? It was unfortunate, but Mr. Becker drowned. I found him myself. He was tangled in the mooring lines of his own boat." I shuddered, remembering how pale his skin had been above his red shirt.

Her eyes danced—she was obviously thrilled to have the upper hand. "Haven't you heard? The police have determined that Declan Becker's death wasn't accidental."

My mind spun out of control. He was murdered? I'd seen the beer bottles on the dock myself. It seemed pretty clear to me that he'd taken his boat out on the Sound, then docked it at the Boathouse and stayed for a few drinks.

"I can't discuss this now."

"Can't you give me some sort of statement?" she wheedled. Niely tugged at my arm again.

"No." I pushed open the door and hastily locked it behind me.

The Boathouse was quiet inside, and I didn't think any of the other staff had arrived yet. I wondered if I should send a text to them to alert them to the reporters outside. When I was out of sight of the front windows, I leaned against the wall and slid to the floor.

Could Declan really have been murdered? Here, on the docks, right outside this building? Obviously, I felt bad for Declan's family and for him, of course, but I couldn't help but wonder how this would affect the Boathouse. The event center was Beth and Lincoln's livelihood, as well as Adam's and mine, and I didn't know how the bad publicity would affect our bookings. With Adam striking out on his own, we sorely needed the income that I earned from working there. Not to mention, it would always hold a special place in my heart as the location where Adam and I were married.

With my thoughts still swimming around me, I pushed myself up from the ground and walked down the hallway to my office. As I walked, I dialed Desi.

She picked up on the first ring. "Hey, Jill, what's up?"

I didn't take time for pleasantries. "Have you heard anything from Tomàs about Declan's death?"

"No, why?"

"Because there's a passel of reporters here in front of the Boathouse, and they're saying that he was murdered." I heard her suck in her breath.

In a shocked tone, she said, "I hadn't heard anything about that. Why do they think that? He was fine when you left, right?"

"Yeah, at least I think so. Can you maybe ask Tomàs about it?" I sat in my desk chair and pulled my knees up to my chest. Desi's voice sounded far away, even though I knew she was just down the street at her café.

"I'll call him and find out. I'm sure there's a big misunderstanding."

I tried to get through as much work as I could, but thoughts of that fateful rehearsal dinner and Declan storming out of the Boathouse kept reverberating through my mind. Ten minutes later, Desi called me back.

"I talked with Tomàs."

"What did he say?"

She cleared her throat. "The reporters are right. The police have released a statement that Declan died under suspicious circumstances."

I pushed away from my desk. "Why are they saying that?"

"Apparently he had a gash on his head."

"Well that would make sense if he hit his head on the dock or his boat. What makes them think someone killed him?" I tapped my fingers on the arm of the chair.

"Apparently it was 'inconsistent' with an accidental fall." I could hear her making air quotes at the word "inconsistent."

What did this all mean for the Boathouse? Would we be liable for Declan's death? We had allowed him to tie up to our docks and that was where he'd been killed. I made a note to call Beth again and see if I needed to update the insurance company.

The phone on my desk rang, and I told Desi I needed to go.

"Call me back later, ok?" she said. "I want to make sure you're all right."

"I will." I disconnected from the phone call with her and picked up the landline phone's receiver.

"Hi, this is Lily Choi from the *Seattle Times*. I was hoping you might have time to answer a few questions for us."

"What do you have questions about?" I was afraid I already knew, but I needed to first make sure that this wasn't regarding any Boathouse business.

"I was hoping you might know something about the death of Declan Becker. Did you know the deceased? Was he a client?"

"No comment." I set the phone back in its cradle. It rang again immediately. I went through the same routine with another reporter. As soon as I hung up from that call, the phone rang again. I pushed the button to send all calls to voicemail. I figured if somebody wanted us for actual Boathouse business, they would leave a message. Right now, I couldn't deal with any more reporters.

Someone knocked on my door. I stared at it, wondering who it could be. The staff wasn't due to arrive yet. Could one of the reporters have managed to get into the Boathouse somehow?

I tiptoed over to the door and opened it slowly, afraid that there might be a long line of reporters in the hallway.

"Oh, it's just you." I stepped aside to allow Desi to enter my office. She held out both hands. In them, she clutched a bag that I hoped contained something sugary and a to-go cup of coffee.

"I thought you might need these. You sounded really stressed on the phone."

"I am." I chomped down on one of the powdered sugar jelly donuts she'd brought for me, savoring the rush of comforting carbohydrates. When I'd finished the first donut, I wiped my face with a napkin and said, "Your mom goes away and everything falls apart. What's it going to be like when she cuts back on her hours on a regular basis?"

Desi laughed and scrunched up her face. "I don't think these are ordinary circumstances. It's not every day that there's a murder investigation going on in Ericksville." She reconsidered her statement. "Well, more than you'd think, but not focusing on the Boathouse."

I sipped the coffee she'd brought. "I've had two reporters call already. This isn't going to go away any time soon, at least not as long as people think there's a murderer on the loose."

"I'm sure it will blow over quickly." She didn't sound terribly confident. "Is there anything I can do to help?"

I thought for a moment. "There is something."

It was one of the last places I wanted to go, but I needed to speak with Becca and Bill about a few details for their wedding—if they still intended to have it.

"Can you go with me out to the cabin on Lake Elinor? I have to talk to Becca, and I don't think she's fond of me at the moment for ruining her rehearsal dinner. You can be my buffer."

She appeared to mentally assess her day and consulted her watch. "I guess I can see if Andrea can stay longer at the café. I *would* like to give Lindsay my condolences about Declan's death. They may not have been on the best of terms recently, but they were married for close to ten years."

"Thanks." I smiled gratefully at her. "I was thinking we could leave in two hours? Does that work for you?"

"Perfect." She hugged me. "Don't worry. It will all turn out ok. It always does."

"Thanks, Desi. I'll call Becca and let her know we're coming."

She turned and left, leaving me alone in my office. I wasn't so sure everything would be ok this time. When our current and prospective clients got wind of the murder investigation, who knew what they'd do?

9

$\mathscr{I}$ stopped to pick Desi up at the café two hours later, and she climbed into my car while handing me another cup of coffee. Although the weather was warm, the intrusion of reporters had chilled me.

"You know me so well," I said, sipping it gratefully. "But you may be enabling my caffeine addiction."

"There are worse things." She grinned and sipped her own drink.

"Do you think Lindsay will be devastated by Declan's death?"

Desi leaned back in her seat and fidgeted with the headrest behind her. "I don't know; it's hard to tell. They've always had such a rocky relationship. But they were married for a long time, so I would think it's affecting her at least a little bit."

"Do you think that the publicity surrounding Declan's death at the Boathouse will die down soon?" I flipped on my turn signal and pulled onto the freeway on-ramp.

"I don't know that either. I hope so." Desi stared out the window. "Can we talk about something else?"

In my tizzy about how the bad press would affect my immediate family and my livelihood, I hadn't given much consideration to how it would affect my sister-in-law. The Boathouse had been a big part of Desi's life from childhood, and she'd only recently given up her part-time position there to go full-time at the BeansTalk Café.

"Did I tell you that Nancy Davenport e-mailed me this week?" Out of the corner of my eye, I saw her turn sharply toward me.

"No, you didn't." She gulped her iced coffee. "What did she want?"

I sighed. "I guess I volunteered to help lead a summer camp next week. I'd totally forgotten about it until she reminded me."

"Whoa. That's not great timing. Do you think she could find somebody else to do it?"

"Do something nice for somebody else?" I laughed. "That's not really in Nancy's wheelhouse. I did ask though. I pretty much got laughed out of the room."

"Ouch." She was silent for a moment. "Are you sure you don't need any help with Becca and Bill's wedding? After all, they are my friends. I'd be happy to help with whatever you need."

I wasn't sure that I didn't need her assistance, but I didn't want to impose on Desi either.

"I'm sure it will be fine." I changed the subject, and we talked about our kids for the rest of the way out to Lake Elinor.

When we pulled up in the driveway, there were several cars at the cabin that I recognized from before. It looked like there was a full crew at the house. Above us, a slight breeze blew fluffy clouds across the sky. Far off in the distance, somewhere on the other side of Puget Sound, ominous dark spots obscured any sign of blue sky. I hoped we'd be home by the time the storm hit Ericksville. We knocked on the door and Becca answered it. Her eyes were puffy and swollen, and she seemed puzzled to see us there.

I smiled at her. "No, we didn't have plans—I just thought I would stop by and confirm a few details with you and Bill."

She raised her eyebrows but recovered quickly. "Sure, that's fine. Everyone's out on the deck. We're all in shock about what happened to Declan. I have to warn you, Lindsay isn't taking it well." She shook her head. "I just can't believe it."

Desi elbowed me as we walked into the house. "You never told her we were coming, did you?"

"No, I forgot. Do you think she's mad that we just stopped by?" I didn't want to tell Desi that I needed to find out if the wedding was still on.

"No, I don't think they care, but it's not like we would just drop by Lake Elinor. It was a forty-five minute drive from Ericksville."

As we had the first day I met Becca, we followed her through the spotless house onto the back deck. However, the mood today was much more somber. Bill and Jared were deep in conversation near the deck railing. They gave no indication they'd noticed our arrival. I didn't see Isabel today, but Orson was sitting in a patio chair near the fire pit. He looked up and waved at us. Lindsay was busy pouring herself a drink at a bar that hadn't been present the last time I'd been there. When she saw Desi and me, she clenched her drink and stumbled toward us. It obviously wasn't her first alcoholic beverage of the day.

Desi and I looked at each other. "I guess Declan's death affected her more than I figured it would," she said in a whisper.

"Yeah, no kidding." I pasted a sympathetic smile on my face as Lindsay approached us.

The expression on her face was anything but pleasant. "What are you two doing here?"

"I had a few things to go over with Becca, and Desi wanted to see all of you." I made an effort to keep my words peaceful and unprovocative.

"Haven't you done enough?" Lindsay's drink sloshed a little as she brought it to her mouth and drank deeply from it. "We attend one dinner at your event center, and now my husband is dead."

I noticed she called him her husband, and not her ex-husband as she had on previous occasions. I wondered if his death had brought about a change of heart. Or maybe it was just the alcohol talking.

I looked around, but Becca had gone inside the house for something. Desi and I were left alone with Lindsay. We stared at each other in awkward silence until Desi spoke.

"Lindsay, I wanted to let you know how sorry I am about Declan. Truly, if there's anything I can do to help, let me know."

The widow glared at us. "I don't need your condolences. I don't know what my husband was doing there at the Boathouse so late, but I do know that your dock is a safety hazard, and I intend to speak to my lawyers about it."

Bill came up behind Lindsay and placed his hand on her shoulder. She shrugged it off, but her scowl decreased by a notch.

"Lindsay's been through quite a shock. We all have." He shook his head. "I still can't believe he's gone."

She looked at him gratefully then swigged from her drink again.

"I'm sure Lindsay realizes that this wasn't your fault or

caused in any way by your business." He turned toward her again. "The police have determined that Declan's death was caused by another person. It wasn't anything to do with the event center."

"We'll see about that," Lindsay said. "If he hadn't taken his boat out there, this never would've happened to him. It was probably some random act of violence, and he was caught up in it."

I was probably poking the bear, but I had to know. "Why did Declan move his boat out there so late at night? I don't remember seeing it there the day before."

Desi nodded her head in agreement. "I didn't see it either." She touched my arm. "I'm going to go say hi to Jared, ok?"

I nodded. She walked away and I turned back to Bill and Lindsay.

Lindsay blushed, whether from the alcohol or from uncertainty, and said, "I'm not sure when, but if he hadn't been drinking after that debacle of a rehearsal dinner, I'm sure he never would've brought the boat out there last night. It's all your fault."

I stared her straight in the eyes. "Wasn't Declan arguing with some woman in the parking lot before the rehearsal dinner?"

Lindsay looked up sharply. "He was. Janelle Dixon. How did you know?"

I shrugged. "Oh, someone told me about it." I didn't want to tell her that someone was me or she'd think I'd been spying on her.

Bill's face blanched. "Janelle? What was Janelle doing there at the Boathouse?

"Who's Janelle?" Desi asked as she rejoined our conversation.

They ignored her.

"I don't know why she was there. How would I know?" Lindsay slurped down the remains of her drink and stomped off toward the bar cart.

I wondered if anyone had told the police about the woman in the parking lot. In all the chaos surrounding the discovery of Declan's body, I hadn't remembered it. Now I wondered if it was even important. Lindsay didn't seem terribly concerned, and Bill didn't seem to know anything about it. However, judging by his reaction, he knew Janelle.

"Bill, who is Janelle?" I watched his face closely.

He shifted a little and ran his fingers along the condensation on the outer rim of his highball glass.

"Janelle went to dentistry school with Declan, Jared, and me. We'd planned for the four of us to start our own dentistry practice after graduation. But, right before we graduated, Declan decided that he didn't want Janelle to be part of our practice."

"Why not?" Desi tilted her head to the side and stared at him. Evidently, she'd never heard this story before.

"I don't know, he never really said. But he was quite adamant about it, so Jared and I gave in."

"That must've been devastating for Janelle," I observed.

He sighed and his gaze shifted to the wood planking of the deck. "I'm sure it was. I never intended to hurt her, but Declan and I had been friends for years before I even met her. When he decided that he didn't want her to be part of the practice, I had to go along with it."

A thought occurred to me. "Was he dating Janelle at the time?" Could his abrupt reversal be due to a lover's quarrel?

"No, he was already dating Lindsay. And he was faithful to her in the beginning." He shook his head. "It wasn't until he became more successful that his attention wandered." His eyes clouded over as though he were remembering that long-ago decision to oust Janelle. "In fact, it may have been Lindsay's influence that caused him to not want to include Janelle in the practice."

"So Lindsay didn't like Janelle?"

Bill never had a chance to answer my question because Becca came out of the house and stood next to us, holding a glass of red wine. I felt her eyes on me, but then she turned to her fiancé.

"Bill!" she admonished. "You never offered our guests anything to drink."

He blushed slightly, but the sadness remained in his eyes. "I'm so sorry. Would you two like anything to drink?"

Desi and I exchanged glances. "Water would be great for both of us," I said.

Relief crossed his face, as if he was glad to have an excuse to leave our conversation. I felt a twinge of remorse to have caused him even more pain so soon after the death of his longtime friend.

"Two waters coming up." The deck vibrated as he strode off toward the bar cart. Lindsay had finished pouring her drink and was now sitting close to Orson on the outdoor love seat, deep in conversation.

Becca smiled at her fiancé, her gaze full of love. "That man, I swear. He's a brilliant dentist, but I've got to work with him on his hosting skills." She turned her attention back to us. "So what did you need to discuss?"

"I hoped to go over some of the wedding details with you and Bill."

Her face lit up. "Sure—with everything going on, I could use a distraction. There's nothing I like better than to review the details. I want this wedding to be perfect." Her face clouded over. "Well, as close to perfect as it can be after what happened to Declan."

"That's actually what I wanted to discuss with you. It would be perfectly understandable if you decided not to go through with the wedding next week."

She fiercely shook her head. "No. Declan would want us to get married. He often teased us about when we'd finally tie the knot. We talked with Lindsay about it and have decided that as soon as Bill and I get back from our honeymoon, we're going to have a memorial service for him, then take his boat out on Puget Sound and scatter his ashes." Her lips quivered.

I nodded. "That sounds like a lovely tribute. But please let me know if you have any concerns about going ahead with your wedding. I want to make sure this is a special day for you and Bill."

"I do too." She looked close to tears.

I patted her arm. "We're going to make sure everything goes smoothly." I mentally crossed my fingers. "I'm really sorry about the seating mix-up at the rehearsal dinner. But if you still intend to go through with the wedding, I do have some details to review with you."

Becca nodded at me, tight-lipped.

Bill returned with our waters.

"Thanks." Desi smiled at him.

"Yes, thank you." I gestured to the house. "Becca and I are going to go over some of the wedding details if you'd like to join us."

He held up his hand. "I think Becca's got it under control." He leaned down and kissed the top of her head. "I'll leave the decision-making to her at this point."

I disappeared into the house with the bride-to-be, leaving Desi talking with Bill on the deck.

Becca and I hammered out the remaining details until I was satisfied that we'd discussed everything and the event would be as perfect as she envisioned. I had taken copious notes in my spiral notebook and intended to copy everything to my computer files as soon as I returned to the Boathouse. I wasn't taking any chances this time.

We returned to the deck. Desi stood alone at the deck railing, while Bill was talking to Lindsay in heated tones. Orson watched the two of them from a nearby chair. Jared was nowhere to be seen.

I tapped Desi on the shoulder and she turned. Her expression was ashen.

"What's wrong?"

Her voice was filled with held-back tears. "Lindsay was horrid to me. She told me she's going to sue the Boathouse and everyone in our family for Declan's death. She's sure it had something to do with him leaving the rehearsal dinner drunk."

"But we didn't overserve him—I saw him pull a flask out of his pocket a few times. And, somehow, he got ahold of a six-pack of beer."

"Yeah, well, tell that to Lindsay. She seems intent on ruining our family business. If the press gets wind of this..." A tear slipped down her face, and she brushed it away before forcing a smile. "Are you ready to go? I don't think I can stay here much longer."

I wrapped my arm around her and squeezed her shoulders. I hated to see her so upset over being hurt by someone she'd considered a friend. We both gazed out at the lake for a minute. The wind had picked up and whitecaps had formed on the water's surface, making globs of algae bob under the water, an eerie reminder of Declan's body floating next to the Boathouse's dock. I shuddered and turned away.

"Let's go. I wanted to get home before the storm anyway."

We got into the car just as the sky opened up and buckets of rain poured down. The friendly cotton-puff clouds from this morning had completely disappeared, replaced by swirling gray clouds as dark as my thoughts. The casual days of drinks on the sunny deck had come to an end.

10

$\mathcal{I}$ hadn't planned on working over the weekend, but since Beth was gone, I had to cover her events as well as mine. On the agenda for Saturday was a baby shower, and on Sunday we had a seventieth birthday party in the evening. I was fairly confident in my abilities to manage both events. I'd done several of them over the past few months and had conferred with Beth the night before about the weekend's plans. I was determined to not let any thoughts of Declan's murder interfere with my duties. At least the reporters were gone, chasing the next ambulance.

As soon as the guest of honor walked in, looking like she was ten months pregnant, my mind switched to active management. The event was an evening baby shower for both the mother- and the father-to-be. About forty guests were scheduled to be in attendance. By the time all the guests had arrived, the tables I'd had the staff set up against the wall groaned under the weight of the baby gifts.

The event went smoothly, and all of the guests were smiling and chattering in small groups as they left. The father-to-be and his father took one load of gifts to the car, then stopped to chat with some of their relatives in the Boathouse's lobby. After carrying the second load of gifts to the car, the father-to-be returned alone, his face as red as a ripe strawberry.

He stormed up to me, looking like he was about to blow. "Somebody stole our baby gifts out of the trunk of my car. Who would have done such a thing?"

My heart raced. Nothing like this had ever happened before at the Boathouse. At least that I knew of. I wasn't sure what Beth would want me to do in this situation, so I did the only thing I could do—apologize.

"I'm so sorry. That's awful." I peered out the front door window. The sky was darkening, and the client's car was one of only a few left in the parking lot. It was parked close to the main sidewalk and against the curb.

His wife waddled up to us and tugged at his arm. "Dylan, what's going on?"

He turned to look at her, his expression softening, and he put his hands on her shoulders. "Honey, I'm sorry, but someone took some of the gifts out of the car."

"What? You mean they stole them?" She ran to the door. "I hope it wasn't the rocking chair from Aunt Linda. It was so beautiful."

"It's still over there." He pointed to the wall and the tables, which were now only half-full.

"Thank goodness." She rubbed her belly. "But what did they take?"

"I don't know," he said grimly. "But this is ridiculous. This is supposed to be a safe neighborhood."

I walked with them out to his Ford Explorer, where his father now stood guard. The tailgate was up, and only a few gifts were left in the truck. The woman started crying.

Her husband wrapped his arms around her and pulled her close. "It's ok, I'm sure they'll turn up."

With his wife's face buried against his chest, he glared at me. I shrank back. It wasn't like it was my fault that his gifts had been stolen. I felt bad, but it probably hadn't been the smartest thing to leave the car unlocked and the tailgate open, especially with darkness setting in to conceal any wrongdoings. Ericksville was generally a safe town, but there were dishonest and evil people everywhere. Declan's murder had proven that. Still, it was a horrible thing to experience. When someone had broken into my house in the spring, the sense of violation had been worse than the damage caused to our house.

"I'll call the police and let them know about the theft," I said. "Maybe they'll be able to locate the gifts." I didn't really believe that, but I felt like I needed to say something comforting to them.

A gust of wind off the water blew past us, carrying the odor of an overflowing trash can in Lighthouse Park. The pregnant woman wrinkled her nose and turned green.

"I need to go inside." She tugged at her husband's arm.

He nodded, and hand-in-hand, they followed me back inside to my office. I called the police, and they told me they would send somebody over to take statements. While we were waiting, the pregnant woman went over to stand with her sister, who had arranged to have the event at the Boathouse.

Whether she knew I was in earshot or not, the sister said loudly, "They clearly need to hire security for these events. I'm going to warn everyone I know to stay away from this part of town until things calm down."

I ducked back around the corner into the hallway near my office, my heart pounding. My worst fears had been confirmed. The bad publicity surrounding Declan's murder had reached our clients.

The police came and talked to the parents-to-be. They took detailed notes about what was missing, but I could tell from their demeanor that they didn't expect to recover any of the stolen goods.

While the family milled around the lobby clearing out the rest of their belongings, I met with the police officer in my office.

"Do you think there's any chance the stolen gifts will be found?"

"We'll certainly do our best, ma'am, but most likely not. I'm sorry."

"Do you think this could have anything to do with the man's body that was found by our docks?"

He shook his head. "I can't say much about that case, but what I can say is that, statistically, most murders aren't random acts of violence—they're carried out by someone the victim knew."

I felt as though someone had dumped a bucket of ice over me. Someone Declan knew. In all likelihood, that meant one of the other people who had attended the rehearsal dinner. Desi's friends.

"Thank you." I stood from my desk. "Will you let me know if you find anything out about the stolen gifts?"

"We will."

Finally, all of the guests left, and I had a chance to check my e-mail and the few voicemails that had come in while I was working the baby shower. There was nothing major in my e-mail, but I listened to the voicemails, hanging up as soon as I heard them. Both of the messages were notifications from booked clients that they were canceling their events at the Boathouse. I called each of them back to plead with them to reconsider, but even with my offer of added security for the event, they opted to cancel. The impact of having a guest murdered on site was becoming apparent. If we couldn't end the negative publicity soon, the business could be in serious financial trouble. This end of the summer season was one of our busiest times of the year, and if we lost too many clients it could be devastating.

I stared at the wall. The only way to fix this mess was for Declan's murderer to be caught, and the Boathouse to be out of the public eye—at least in a negative context. The police didn't seem to be making much progress in the case, at least that I knew of. I'd met most of the people that Declan had been around the day of his murder, so I figured I could probably find something out that could lead the police in the right direction. After all, I had done some sleuthing in the past that had helped bring some very bad people to justice. Being the events coordinator at the Boathouse gave me an in with Declan's crowd that the police didn't have. And Desi could easily infiltrate them to snoop a little too.

Satisfied with my plan, I finished up my work for the day and headed home. I wasn't looking forward to telling Beth about the stolen baby gifts, but it didn't seem major, so I left it for the next day.

11

I spent Sunday managing a successful seventieth birthday party and breaking the news to Beth about the stolen baby gifts, which she took surprisingly well. By Monday, I was eager to start trying to figure out if one of Declan's friends had killed him. If the murderer wasn't caught soon, the Boathouse would stay in the media spotlight and there might not be a business for Lincoln and Beth to come home to. As soon as I got into my office, I began a list of possible suspects. Unless Declan's death had been a random act of violence, which the police officer I'd spoken to had deemed unlikely, the murderer was probably one of the group staying at the cabin on Lake Elinor with him or the woman he'd argued with on the day he died.

1) Janelle Dixon – hated Declan because he wouldn't allow her to be a partner in their dental practice

2) Bill Friede – Declan and Jared's partner in the dental practice—seemed too nice, but appearances could be deceiving

3) Becca Liu – Declan and Lindsay's divorce ruining her

wedding seemed a bit of a stretch for murder, but I left her on there for consistency

4) Jared Seely– Declan and Bill's partner in the dental practice—why would he have killed his partner?

5) Lindsay Becker – going through a bitter divorce with Declan

6) Isabel Liu – Becca's cousin—I wasn't sure what relationship, if any, she had with the rest of the group

Declan had argued with Janelle Dixon the day he died, so she seemed like a good place to start. I looked her up on the internet and found that she worked as a dentist for low-income children in nearby Everton. I had about ninety minutes until I needed to be at the preschool for summer camp, and I'd intended to visit the Boathouse's florist in Everton sometime soon, so I figured I could combine the visits. But how was I going to approach Janelle? I didn't have any reason to visit her or her office.

I had to have some sort of excuse to see her—maybe a claim that I'd found something of hers. I looked around the room for something I could use as a prop and spotted my sunglasses on the edge of the desk. They were my favorites —the only designer brand item I owned, and I hoped she wouldn't tell me they actually were hers because I didn't want to lose them. The sun shone brightly, and I slipped the sunglasses on for the drive over to Janelle's office.

I drove into the parking lot of her dental practice and parked next to a beat-up Honda Civic. The first thing I did was to duck down in the seat and remove my sunglasses. Before going into the building, I stood in front of my car for a minute working up the nerve to enter. If Janelle had killed Declan, this probably wasn't the smartest thing to do, but it was my best lead at the moment.

Her dental office, which appeared to be shared with two

other dentists, was in an old one-story brown house off the main road. The exterior had been livened up with a colorful rainbow sign with children on it and the name of the practice. I was about to turn the doorknob, when the door swung open and someone walked out toward the Honda. It was the same woman with frizzy dishwater blonde hair that I'd seen arguing with Declan in the parking lot of the Boathouse— Janelle Dixon.

I pasted a smile on my face. "Hi, are you Janelle?"

"Yes, why? Did you have an appointment today?" She cocked her head to the side and scanned my car, as if searching for a child in need of dental care.

"No, I'm actually here for something else." I held up the sunglasses. "Are these yours?"

She reached into her purse and felt around. "No, mine are right here." She extracted a pair of silver-toné sunglasses. "Those look awfully expensive. Where did you find them? Did someone tell you they were mine?"

"I work at the Boathouse in downtown Ericksville. We found these in the parking lot, and someone remembered seeing you talk to one of our guests out there that day." I checked her face to gauge her reaction.

She flushed a little. "I was in Ericksville last week to go jogging along the waterfront, but I don't remember talking to anyone in the Boathouse parking lot. Anyway, they're not mine, but thanks for coming here to ask me." She looked at me with curiosity. "Who was it that told you they were mine?"

A police car's lights flashed and its sirens blared as it raced by on the next street over, giving me a chance to think about whether or not to tell her it had been Lindsay.

"Oh, one of our clients." I hesitated. Should I tell her

who had mentioned her name? Lindsay wasn't technically our client, so it was probably ok.

"Actually, it was Lindsay Becker. Do you know her?"

Janelle's face darkened and she scowled. "I do. I remember now. I spoke with Lindsay's husband, Declan."

"Yeah, she said you were old friends." I didn't think it was my business to tell her about Declan's death, and besides, if I did so, she might not be so forthcoming with me about her relationship with him. I leaned against my car, then thought better of it when the hot metal burned through my dress pants.

She scoffed. "She said we were friends?"

I nodded. "Yes."

She shifted her weight from foot to foot and toed the cracked blacktop. "That's rich."

I smiled companionably. "I take it there's no love lost between the two of you. I have to say I haven't found Lindsay very pleasant to work with either, so I don't blame you."

"That woman is a real witch, if you know what I mean." Fire burned in her eyes.

"I see you're a dentist. Is that how you know Declan?"

"Yes. I went to dental college with Declan, Bill, and Jared. Do you know them?" She continued without waiting for my response. "They have a dental practice together." She sighed. "The plan was always for the four of us to open our own practice after school. Unfortunately, Queen Lindsay didn't like that plan. I think she was jealous and didn't want me anywhere near Declan. She put her foot down and told them she didn't want me there. The guys had been friends for a while, so I didn't have much of a chance of changing their minds."

"Ooh," I said, "that's horrible. Did they tell you it was Lindsay's fault?"

"Bill told me." Her lips quivered. "He always was the nicest of them. I could tell he felt really bad about the decision the others had made."

She looked at her watch. "You know, at the time, I thought that all my dreams for the future were over. Now, I know I was meant for other things." She motioned to the dental office. "If I stayed with those three, I wouldn't have had the opportunity to help out so many children that desperately need my help. True, I'd probably be rolling in dough right now, but this makes me happy." An optimistic gleam appeared in her eyes. "This was actually the best thing to ever happen to me."

"Well, sometimes these things just work out for the best." I eyed her face for any tells that she wasn't being truthful. There were none that I could see.

"I better get going," she said as she unlocked the door of the beater I'd parked next to.

"Well, even if these weren't your sunglasses, it was nice to meet you. I guess I'll have to put these in the lost and found." I held the sunglasses up in the air.

"Nice to meet you too." She opened her car door and started to climb into the driver's seat.

Something occurred to me. "Wait, why were you and Declan arguing? It sounded like everything between you happened years ago, and you're in a good place now."

She gave a harsh laugh. "A long time ago, when we discussed opening a practice together, I invested some money to start the business. By the time Lindsay managed to get me thrown out of the group, it was too late to recoup my investments—they'd already been spent. They promised me they'd pay me back when they started making money. I'd completely forgotten about it until I saw Declan when I was jogging by the Boathouse last week. I asked him if he could please send me a check for my share. I wasn't asking for anything other than what I'd contributed."

She shook her head. "That jerk had the nerve to tell me that I wasn't getting my money. He said the practice was almost bankrupt. I may not be friends with any of them anymore, but I still hear talk around the dental community. There is no way their practice was hurting for money. If he won't give me back my money, I'm going to have to involve my lawyer." She tapped her watch. "I've really got to get going. It was nice to meet you."

She shut her door and roared away, exhaust belching out of the muffler like a miniature smokestack.

I coughed and waved the exhaust away before putting the sunglasses back on and getting into the car. Janelle seemed to sincerely enjoy her current job, but did that mean she hadn't killed Declan? Money was a powerful motivator, and he had refused to give her what she was owed. Could she have been enraged by his declaration and followed him to the Boathouse last Wednesday night? It seemed a little far-fetched, but having a man murdered at the Boathouse seemed just as strange.

*a*fter a quick chat with the florist, I left Everton for my shift at the preschool. I wasn't looking forward to the parking situation as the lot was rather small, and heaven forbid I park in one of the reserved parking spots. I'd already been chewed out by Nancy for that in the past. When I got there, I was pleased to see fewer cars in the parking lot than usual because it was summer and fewer children were enrolled in summer camp than in regular preschool. Of course, Nancy's van was there.

When I entered the school, I was surprised that they had changed the layout of the classroom since I'd met with Nancy last week. The theme for this week was Sail Away, and someone had taped a giant mural of a seascape on the wall. On the floor, a turquoise-streaked navy blue rug had replaced the ABC rug that the children usually sat on for storytime. A few of the smaller tables had been pushed together to form one large table, and it looked like there was some sort of craft project set up on it.

Children were starting to arrive for the day, including Mikey. Adam had walked over from our house with both of the kids. He held Ella in his arms, and I wondered if he'd left the stroller at home—if so, his arms must be killing him. Mikey saw me and ran over to me.

"Mommy! I missed you this morning." He wrapped his arms around me, his little hands barely reaching my waist.

I kissed him on the forehead. "I missed you too, little bunny. But you got to spend some time with Daddy. Wasn't that nice?"

Mikey grinned. "Yeah. He made us chocolate chip pancakes."

I widened my eyes. "Ooh, lucky! Those sound yummy. I'll have to try those one day."

He nodded. "Daddy said Grandpa Lincoln used to make them for him."

"Ah. Well, good thing the tradition continues." I stood and ran my hand over Ella's gleaming red hair that matched mine. Adam held her in his arms with a pained expression on his face.

"She didn't seem as heavy at home, but by the time we got here I felt like she'd gained twenty pounds."

"You didn't push her in the stroller?" I took her from him.

He stretched out his arms. "No, it didn't seem necessary. I'm regretting that decision now."

I smothered a grin. "That's why I usually use the stroller when we walk to school. Do you want to take my car? I don't need it today, and I could use the exercise from walking home from work."

"That might be best," Adam said, a sheepish smile on his face. I handed him my keys and he shoved them in his pocket.

Mikey tugged on my arm. "Mom, Mom! They're starting."

"Well, you'd better get in there." Adam winked at me and nodded his head at the classroom. "Have fun in there, sweetie. I see they've got some fun crafting on the agenda for you today."

I glared at him and handed Ella back. He wisely took that as his cue to exit. My husband knew me too well. I wasn't fond of craft projects. I'd never been very coordinated, and cutting and gluing things together weren't my strong suits.

I followed Mikey into the classroom. Ms. Shana, Mikey's regular teacher, was leading the summer camp session.

She clapped her hands three times, and the kids followed with three claps of their own. I stared at her, amazed at her ability to control the chaos. I could harely get one kid to be quiet, much less twenty. The other parents, a man and woman who I vaguely recognized from drop-off, had the same expression of awe on their faces as the one I knew was on mine.

"Ok, class, we've got some fun stuff planned for you this week. As you may have guessed, this week is Sail Away summer camp."

"Ooh," they said collectively.

"Are we going on a real boat?" The little girl who'd asked looked like she was about to cry. "I'm afraid of going out on the water."

Ms. Shana patted her arm. "Don't worry, Susie. This is all pretend. We aren't going out on any real boats this week." Susie's smile returned. "The first thing we're going to do today is to make our own wooden sailboats. Then, later in the day, we will float them outside and maybe even have some races." She turned her attention to me and the other two parent volunteers, who were standing nearby, looking just as awkward as I felt. "If I could get two of you to go over to the craft table and one of you to help Ms. Nancy with snack preparation, that would be great."

The other mom jetted off toward the kitchen. Shoot. I'd lost my chance, although snack prep was with Nancy, so maybe crafting was the lesser of the two evils. I shuffled off toward the craft table, trying to put an enthusiastic smile on my face before the children got there. I spent the next hour cutting out sails and decals for the kids to put on their wooden sailboats.

"Miss Jill?" The little girl I'd been helping held up the triangle I'd cut her for a sail. "This doesn't look right."

I examined the cutout. She was right. I hadn't done a very good job of cutting it, and it was rather lopsided. I made her another one, but that still didn't meet her standards. On my fourth attempt, I gritted my teeth and cut the sail as best as I possibly could. Finally, she declared it acceptable and glued it to the mast of her sailboat. I glanced at the clock. Being in the same room with so many demanding preschoolers at a time was making me crazy.

Not any too soon, Nancy called out that it was time for snack. The kids ran back to the kitchen area, where she and the other mom had placed napkins with Pirate's Booty and apple slices on each table. My stomach rumbled. I hadn't had time for breakfast that morning. It looked like there were plenty of apple slices left, so I grabbed one off a plate on the counter. I was taking my first bite when I noticed Nancy glaring at me. I lowered the apple and met her gaze.

"Jill, those are for the kids." I nodded and lowered my hand. I wanted to tell her where she could stick the piece of fruit, but I was on her turf and I didn't want to do anything that would get Mikey in trouble.

After snack, Ms. Shana read stories about boats to the kids, and the dad who had helped me with crafts taught them how to tie a sailor's knot. I wasn't actively involved with any of these activities, so I had time to think about how much coordination was still needed for Bill and Becca's wedding. My stomach started to ache from all the twisting in my guts. Finally, it was almost the end of the summer camp day.

"Ok, kids," Ms. Shana said. "It's time for what you've all been waiting for. We're going to take our sailboats outside and float them in the kiddie pool that Ms. Nancy set up for you."

The four-year-olds bumbled around, trying to locate the sailboats they'd made earlier in the day. Daniel, my friend Dorinda's son, and another little boy were hanging around the Lego bin with their sailboats. I saw the other boy stick a Lego man into his pocket, and they both giggled.

Unfortunately, Nancy saw them too. She was on them before they could wipe the grins off their faces.

"Daniel! Evan! Put those toys back in the bin. This center is closed. You know better than to play with things from a closed activity." She turned to me and ice filled my veins. Being around her was like being back in elementary school and having the teacher reprimand me.

"And you need to be watching them and keeping them on track. It's time for them to be outside with their sailboats now." She shooed them away, first making sure that Evan had replaced the Legos he'd taken.

My mouth dropped. It was one thing to alert me to what she wanted me to do, but it was another to do so in front of the kids. "Really, Nancy?" I said, eyeing her with disdain.

She pursed her lips together. "Maybe you should have been keeping better track of them."

Without another word to her, I swiveled around and nudged the remaining kids outside. They raced to the playground, where Nancy had set up a small kiddie pool and had tied a string across the middle of the pool, bisecting it into two racing lanes.

I divided the kids up into two lines and had them stand next to the pool.

"Cool!" one of the kids said.

Ms. Shana instructed them on how to race their sailboats and then went back inside to prepare for the next day. I stood to the side of the pool, cheering them on. Nancy was at the far side of the playground watching the kids who had completed their races.

A little girl giggled, and I looked down. Daniel was making a Lego pirate jump up and down on the side of his boat.

"Arr, matey, walk the plank." He laughed.

"Where did that toy come from?" I hadn't seen Daniel bring it outside, and I knew Nancy had confiscated Evan's pilfered Legos.

He grinned at me and hid the pirate under a piece of cloth he'd laid across the back of his boat. Then, he gave the boat a shove, sending it spinning off toward the other side of the kiddie pool. I shook my head and glanced around. Nancy wouldn't be very happy if she knew that he had taken Legos outside. The water wasn't going to hurt the plastic toy, though, so I didn't say anything. Plus, I was happy to see Daniel making friends at school now, and I felt a bit rebellious by actively disobeying her.

By the time the last child had finished, parents started to arrive to pick up their children. Mikey was staying in aftercare today because I had to go back in to work. In the past, Beth would watch him after preschool summer camp when Adam needed to work, but she obviously wasn't available now. I really needed to find a babysitter for him and Ella. That task had to go to the top of my priority list.

When I had a free moment at work, I called my in-laws. It wasn't something I had been looking forward to doing, but I had to let them know what was going on at the Boathouse. I knew that the circumstances weren't my fault, but I still felt like they were.

I dialed and held my breath, almost hoping they wouldn't pick up. Lincoln answered his phone on the second ring. I expelled the air in my lungs and greeted him. "Hi."

"Hi, Jill, it's nice to hear from you. How are things going up there?"

"Uh, not so great actually." I rolled a ballpoint pen between my fingers, digging the clip into the pad of my thumb.

"Have things become worse?" Normally, Lincoln was calm in all situations, but now, I heard a tinge of worry in his tone.

"Let me talk to her." Beth's voice came over the line.

"No, Lincoln, don't put Beth on. I don't want to cause her any stress."

I heard a shuffling noise on the other end.

"Jill. What's going on?" she demanded.

I sighed. So much for keeping it from Beth. "Too much. On Saturday someone stole baby gifts out of a client's car in the parking lot. They weren't too happy about it. Now, based on all the bad publicity surrounding Declan's death, we're getting cancellations."

"Cancellations?" she echoed. "How many?"

"Only two so far, but I won't be surprised if there are more. The press has been hanging around, and everyone in the entire area knows what happened here."

Beth was quiet, and then in a steely voice said, "We're coming home." She muffled the phone, but I heard her tell Lincoln to pack their bags.

"You can't come home. You're not supposed to travel long distances yet." Adam would kill me if he found out I was responsible for his mom getting sicker.

"I'm fine," she scoffed.

"No, you're not," said Lincoln, who now had control over the phone. In the background, Beth loudly protested his declaration. "Jill, we're not coming home until next week. But we'll handle calling the insurance company and figure out what we should do. I can't believe this is happening."

I could almost see him shaking his head.

"Ok. I'll send you all the details about the theft and anything else I can think of. Thanks, and I'm really sorry to have to bother you about this."

"It's not a problem. We appreciate you stepping in to help with everything while we're away, and we're confident you'll do great at handling all of this. Right, Beth?" His voice was fainter through the phone line as he talked to his wife.

"Right," she called through the line. "Thanks, Jill. I'll call you tomorrow."

"Bye."

I hung up the phone, relieved to have that distasteful task completed. Thank goodness Beth had come to her senses and realized it wasn't a good idea to travel. Or rather Lincoln had made that decision for both of them. I knew he'd take care of everything on the business end; now it was just up to me to do everything I could to make the negative publicity come to an end.

13

---

*T*uesday morning, I showed up to work extra early. My to-do list was full, and I had to head over to the preschool a few hours later for summer camp. I had managed to check several items off of my list when Desi appeared in the doorway of my office.

"Hey," I said. "What are you doing here? Are you baking this morning?" I nodded in the direction of the kitchen and sniffed the air. I hadn't smelled anything yummy that morning, but maybe she'd gotten a late start. At least, I could hope. A pastry sounded pretty good at the moment.

"No, sorry. But I do have some good news for you." She bounced up and down on the balls of her feet, causing the skirt of her flowing maxi dress to ripple.

I folded my hands in front of me on the desk. "What is it? I could use some good news."

"Jill, Declan didn't drown at the Boathouse." Her eyes gleamed and she tossed her curly hair back from her shoulders.

What was she talking about? Of course Declan had drowned at the Boathouse. As much as I wanted to believe there was a possibility he hadn't, it seemed too coincidental that he could've drowned elsewhere in the Sound and then had his body wash up near the docks of the same place he'd had dinner that night.

"What do you mean?" I leaned forward.

"They found freshwater in his lungs, not saltwater."

"Freshwater? Like from a lake?" That was even stranger. How was it possible that Declan had drowned in a lake and then turned up next to our dock on Puget Sound?

"Yes, a lake. Lake Elinor, to be exact."

"How do they know which lake it was?" This was sounding too good to be true.

"The water in his lungs is an exact match for the water composition and something called the filamentous algae that they have at Lake Elinor. I think it's all that green stuff you see floating in the lake." She grimaced as if remembering how gross the algae looked on the shore.

I sat back in my chair. "Whoa."

"No kidding." Desi put her hand on the back of the chair opposite me. "Now maybe people will stop blaming us for his death."

I thought about what she'd had said about Declan having died at Lake Elinor. "So it's not Janelle." It was unlikely that she would've followed Declan back to Lake Elinor, so I thought it was a safe bet to cross her off my list of suspects.

"Who?" She tilted her head to the side and gave me a questioning look.

"Janelle Dixon. She was supposed to be one of four partners in the dental practice with Declan, Bill, and Jared, but before they opened, Declan vetoed having her be in the partnership."

She nodded. "Oh yeah, I remember you talking to Bill about her. So why would you think she killed him?"

"When your friends got to the Boathouse last Wednesday, I saw Declan arguing with a woman in the parking lot. Lindsay told me her name when we went there on Friday. I may or may not have gone to visit her yesterday to ask her about Declan." I snuck a peek at her.

She sighed. "You were snooping, weren't you? Remember, we promised Tomàs we wouldn't get involved with any other police cases again."

"I just wanted to find out if she had anything to do with Declan's death. But I think she's in the clear if he actually drowned in Lake Elinor."

"I probably would've done the same thing if I'd known about her arguing with Declan. But if she didn't kill him, who did?"

"I think it had to have been one of your friends from college." I watched Desi closely.

Her good mood disappeared. "One of my friends?" The corners of her mouth drooped. "Why does it have to be one of them? I just don't think that's possible."

"Think about it. Who else had access to him at Lake Elinor? It would have been pretty suspicious for Janelle to have gone all the way out there."

She paused in contemplation. "Then how did his boat end up at the Boathouse's dock? And why was Declan's body in Puget Sound? Tomàs said they found his truck and trailer at the Ericksville boat launch parking lot. If Declan didn't drive it there, who did?"

"I don't know." I stared helplessly at her. "None of this makes much sense."

"Well, I don't think it was one of my friends," she said

stubbornly. "It could easily have been someone who killed him at the boat dock."

"I guess so." Based on what the police officer who responded to the baby gift theft had said about the probability of it being someone Declan knew, that seemed unlikely.

Desi checked her watch. "I've got to get to work, but let me know if you find anything else out." She waggled her finger at me. "And don't do any more investigating on your own. It isn't safe."

"Uh, huh," I said dryly. She wasn't above snooping herself.

She gave me a lopsided smile. "Well, at least take me with you then."

So much for not listening to Tomàs's advice to stay out of police business. But then again, it wasn't like she could completely avoid her friends for the rest of her life, right?

"Aye, aye, Captain." I saluted her. Sail Away camp was rubbing off on me. "I'm meeting Becca today after preschool summer camp is over if you'd like to tag along." Usually clients came to our office to discuss their events, but after the snafu with Becca's rehearsal dinner, I was laying out the red carpet for her.

"Huh? Why do you have to wait?"

I scowled and she started laughing.

"Oh yeah, I forgot you were helping with Sail Away camp."

Desi left the office shaking her head and grinning.

While good news; the conversation with Desi hadn't been on my agenda. I was behind on my to-do list and there was one more thing I had to get done before I left for the preschool—find a babysitter.

My friend Brenda had recommended BabySitNW.com,

so I pulled up their website. Images of giggling babies and smiling women, who I assumed represented the babysitters, filled my screen. I completed a short questionnaire and I was officially a member of the site. Now for the hard part— sorting through all the candidates.

There weren't many that I'd give serious consideration. One woman's ad was full of emoticons and misspellings. Another said she'd been convicted of a DUI recently, but it had been years since her previous DUIs. I stared at the screen. If only Beth wasn't sick. From recent experience, I knew far too well how seemingly ordinary people could be hiding dangerous secrets.

I pushed that thought out of my head. I'd always known that I needed to have a backup babysitter for when both Beth and I had to work, but with Adam home more this summer, we'd been able to make it work thus far. Now, it was no longer an option to hold off on hiring someone to watch the kids.

I knocked my forehead against the desk, then sat back and dug in. There had to be someone in here that was trustworthy enough to care for my children. By the time I had to leave for the preschool, my brain was numb, but I'd set up meetings with two prospective babysitters.

I packed up my things and set out for a day of crafts and games. The walk did relieve some of my stress, and it felt good to stretch my legs. I swallowed the last dregs of my coffee, took a deep breath, and entered Busy Bees.

Summer camp wasn't nearly as bad as I'd thought it would be. In fact, I actually had some fun with the day's craft project, a sail with drawings of each child's family members on it. Mikey's was cute, with a picture of Adam and me holding hands with him and Ella. For a few hours, it felt like my life was back to normal.

14

I picked up Desi and drove out to Lake Elinor with her. Now that I was familiar with the route, it seemed like it took less time to get there. Only two cars were in the driveway when we arrived.

"Looks like everyone's gone home for now," I observed.

"Poor Becca. She had wanted this to be a fun week of relaxation for everyone, and nothing is going as she planned." Desi exited the car and shut her door, eyeing the house. "I hope Lindsay isn't here. I don't think I can deal with her anymore."

Unfortunately for Desi, Lindsay opened the door right then.

"Becca's in the living room being fitted for her dress." She disappeared into the house without any type of friendly greeting.

Desi and I looked at each other.

"Well, that was a nice welcome," I said.

"No kidding. Did we do something to make her mad? She has to know by now that the Boathouse had nothing to do with Declan's death."

"I'm pretty sure my existence makes her angry." I frowned, remembering how Lindsay had treated me the last time I'd seen her. "That and I'm pretty sure she still holds us responsible."

We walked into the living room and found Becca standing on a stool with a magnificent white dress trailing to the ground behind her.

"Wow," Desi said, circling her friend. "You look gorgeous. That dress suits you perfectly."

"It's so pretty," I said. The dress was strapless but not low-cut, and had beads on the bodice and flower patterns embroidered on the satin skirt.

Becca beamed. "Thank you. I love it too." She swished side to side, causing the elderly woman who was pinning her dress to sigh in exasperation.

"Sorry, Glenda," Becca said. "Do you know how much longer it'll be until I'm done?"

The seamstress pulled a pin out from between her lips and assessed the dress. "Maybe another ten minutes? Depends on whether you move around like you just did."

"Ok, girls, go ahead and get something to drink. There's chips and dip in the kitchen, too, if you're hungry." She craned her neck around, taking care not to move the dress. "I'm not sure where Lindsay went. As soon as I'm done here, we can talk, ok?"

I froze in place. She'd told me before that she wasn't planning on canceling their wedding at the Boathouse, but her words still turned my stomach into a pit of dread. We couldn't afford to lose any more business.

"Jill," Desi said, her hand on my arm. "Let's go grab something to drink."

When we were alone in the kitchen, she turned to me and said, "What's going on? You were a statue in there. I thought I'd have to throw cold water on you to get you to move."

Heat rose up through my shoulders and neck. "It's all the cancellations. They're making me crazy." I looked directly into her eyes. "You don't think Becca and Bill will cancel, do you?"

"No, no. Don't worry. If they haven't said anything by now, they're not going to, ok?"

Her words were mildly comforting.

"Now, let's get something to drink. Do you want water? Coffee?" She opened the refrigerator. "There's soda pop in here too." She twisted a can of Diet Pepsi in the air. "I know you want some more caffeine."

I held my hand out. "Thanks."

She took another can of Diet Pepsi out and popped open the tab. It sprayed up in the air and down her arm. "Ugh. It got on my shirt. I love this shirt." She pouted and held up the edge of her off-white lace-trimmed blouse.

"Maybe Becca has some stain remover in the laundry room?"

"I hope so." Desi went off down the hallway, leaving me alone in the kitchen, staring at my drink.

"I told her not to have the wedding at the Boathouse," Lindsay said from behind me.

I swiveled around. "I'm sorry, I don't understand."

"I told Becca not to have it there in the first place. It's a second-rate place in a rinky-dink town. But she insisted because of Desi's connection to it." She leaned against the doorframe, resting her wine glass on the counter.

My jaw dropped. The Boathouse was consistently ranked as one of the hottest places to have a wedding in all of Puget Sound, including much more expensive locations in Seattle.

"I'm sorry you feel that way," I said in even tones. My long-ago yoga instructor would have been proud of me.

"Well, I'm not going to let anyone else get stuck having an event at your establishment." She twisted her lips into an evil smile. "I plan to tell everyone I know to avoid it at any cost, including my aunt at the KINO news station."

Her words echoed in my mind. Her aunt at KINO? If her aunt had any power there, that could bring some seriously bad publicity slamming down on the Boathouse.

"Why would you do that?" I couldn't understand how anyone could be so vindictive.

"Because my husband died there."

I didn't bother to correct her. He'd actually died at Lake Elinor, and she was most likely one of the police's prime suspects. She certainly was high on my suspect list. As such, why was I alone in the kitchen with her?

"Excuse me." Without another word, I turned and, with my head high, walked in the direction Desi had gone.

After a few wrong turns in the massive house, I found Desi scrubbing away at her shirt in a spotless laundry room.

"I think it's coming off," she said with a smile.

"I just had a conversation with Lindsay," I said.

Desi stopped mid-dab and met my eyes. "Oh? Was it bad? What did she say?"

"Basically that she wants to ruin us."

Her lips formed an O. "I don't understand what's going on with her. I mean, Lindsay's always thought a lot of herself, but she didn't use to be this vindictive."

Becca appeared in the doorway. "Hey, I thought I heard voices down here." Her eyes caught on Desi's shirt. "What happened?"

"I fought a Diet Pepsi and it won," Desi quipped.

"Do you want to borrow something to wear?" Becca asked.

"No, I think I'm done. This material dries quickly." Desi dropped the hem of her shirt and replaced the sponge and stain remover.

"Ok, then let's go back to the living room, and we can talk about the wedding plans."

Back in the living room, I sat on one of the long over-stuffed couches and Desi sat on the other end. Becca perched on the edge of an armchair. Her mood was somber, and fear filled me again.

"I wanted to talk to you about changing the catering."

"The catering?" I sighed with relief, which I hoped she hadn't taken as exasperation.

"Yes. Instead of a buffet, I'd like for dinner to be served to each guest at their table."

"Ok." She didn't seem to have noticed my sigh. While not as bad as canceling the event, this last-minute change would put a kink in the event plans. I'd have to change the staff schedule to accommodate the need for more servers, and we'd need to shift around some other supplies. I made a note to ask Lizzie to work on that.

"Sure," I said finally. "Did you want the same menu?"

She squirmed a little. "I would like to have risotto instead of the rice pilaf. Is that possible?"

I breathed another sigh of relief and smiled at her. If she'd changed the entree, I didn't know what I would have told her. "Risotto will be fine." I made the changes in my notebook and set an alert on my phone to remember to tell the kitchen staff of the change.

"Great!" she said brightly. "That was it."

Desi shot me an "I told you so" glance. I shrugged. With the way things were going, nothing would surprise me now.

Becca had opened the curtains, and I saw a car pull up to the driveway. The front door slammed shut before the car door was open. I got up to see who had just arrived. Lindsay approached the vehicle. Jared got out and stood about a foot away from her, leaning against the hood of the car.

Their conversation didn't look like a friendly social encounter. Lindsay's face grew more and more animated, and she waved her hands around in the air as she spoke. I couldn't hear what they were saying, but Jared seemed like he was getting angry with her. Neither of them looked up toward the house. Finally, he brushed past her and came into the house.

Becca and Desi had joined me at the window. We all quickly sat back down in our seats to pretend as though we'd been there all along.

Lindsay's voice drifted into the living room from the entry hall. "I'm not done talking to you."

"Well, I've told you. Declan's share of the practice wasn't worth anything. There's no money."

"You're lying."

"I'm done with this. If you don't believe me, fine."

A minute later, Jared entered the living room with a smile on his face. "Good afternoon."

"Hey," Becca said nonchalantly. "We were just chatting about the wedding plans. I've decided to have a more formal dinner."

He nodded, obviously not interested. "Great, great. Well, I just wanted to say hi. It's been a long day. I think I'm going to rest for a while before dinner."

"Sounds good," Becca said.

We watched him leave the room.

"What was that all about?" Desi leaned toward Becca. "Why was Lindsay so mad at him?"

"I don't know." Becca shook her head. "I'm sure the dental practice is fine. Bill would have told me if they were having financial difficulties." She lowered her voice to a whisper. "Lindsay's been worrying about money for a while though, even before Declan died."

Desi and I moved closer to her.

"Wouldn't she get half of everything in the divorce?" I asked.

"No," Becca said. "They had a prenuptial agreement. Declan never did trust that she wasn't after his money." She pursed her lips. "Lindsay would have received nothing if they divorced. She had her lawyers fighting the prenup, but she lost the case last week. However, she told me he never updated his will. She's still his sole heir."

Desi nudged me and I elbowed her back. I could tell she wanted me to pry into it further.

"So now that Declan is dead, Lindsay gets everything," I said slowly.

"Right." Becca stared straight ahead. "Everything."

We were all quiet.

"That's a pretty good motive for murder," Desi said.

Becca put her head in her hands. "This was supposed to be the perfect pre-wedding vacation. Now I may have a murderer staying here with me. I can't believe it could be one of our friends. I just don't think any of them could do that to Declan."

"Who could do what?" A voice asked from the hallway.

Our heads shot up. Lindsay.

"Who could I have make the first toast," Becca said smoothly. "I'm thinking Desi, as the matron of honor."

Lindsay glared at Desi. Well, at least I wasn't the only one on her naughty list.

"I should go first. I already have my toast prepared."

"I think she should go first," Desi said.

Becca appeared to be considering it. "That will work out well then."

Lindsay nodded and continued down the hallway.

Becca stood from the armchair. "How about we all go out on the deck now? I'd love some fresh air after that long dress-fitting session."

"We should be going," Desi said. "Jill and I need to pick up our kids from preschool."

"Sure. Next time bring the little guys. I'd love to meet them."

I looked around the room. Most of the furniture was light-colored and the carpet was pristine. "I'm not sure you want our boys here."

Becca laughed. "This place has seen worse. Remember, my brothers and I came here every summer when we were kids."

"I'll make sure to bring Anthony next time I see you." Desi smiled at her. "Actually, next time I see you will probably be at the wedding." She hugged her old friend. "You're going to be a beautiful bride, and the wedding will be perfect. Jill will make sure of that, right, Jill?"

I nodded. "I've got your requests on file and will brief the staff. Everything will be wonderful."

"I hope so." Becca's smile faded. "Bill still needs to find another groomsman, and Lindsay is losing it. I don't know if we'll make it to the wedding. I guess there's always elopement."

"Becca! Don't worry." Desi hugged her again and backed out into the hallway. "C'mon, Jill, we've got to go."

I didn't need to be told twice. Between the shadow of Declan's murder and Lindsay's mood swings, the house had a bad vibe. Becca walked us out and waved goodbye.

On the way home, I felt myself relax. "I hadn't realized how stressed that house made me feel," I said.

"Me neither." Desi shuddered. "I'm starting to think Lindsay is a little upset that Becca made me her matron of honor instead of her."

"Ya think?" I laughed. "Her eyes were shooting daggers into your skull when Becca talked about having you lead the toasting."

"They have been closer in recent years. I've been out of touch since getting married and then having the kids. I think Becca chose me though because we were roommates so long. We were quite close back then." She looked wistful.

"Has Lindsay always been like this?"

"No. Even compared to earlier in the week, she's become more unhinged."

"Unhinged enough to have murdered her husband?"

"I don't know." Desi rummaged through her purse and pulled out a bar of chocolate. "Want half?"

My stomach grumbled. We'd never eaten the snacks Becca had offered. And she was offering me chocolate. Enough said.

15

I'd set up interviews with two babysitters who looked promising and had arranged to meet them at the BeansTalk Café.

"You look prepared." Desi gestured to the two notebooks I held in my hands.

"I want to make sure I select the right person to take care of Mikey and Ella."

"Ok, no judgment. I went through the same thing when we were looking for someone to help out. Luckily, the neighbor girl is usually available when my parents or the in-laws can't watch the kids."

"I wish my parents lived closer." Then again, I wasn't sure I did want them to live near us. In June, my parents had announced their intention to separate after over thirty years of marriage. Their declaration had hurt, and as much as I tried to be ok with it, I was happy to have many miles distancing me from having to see them apart.

"What time is the first person supposed to be here?"

I looked at my watch. "In about five minutes. Can I please have a cup of coffee and a cherry Danish to eat here?"

She rang me up and then set a piping hot mug of coffee and a plated pastry on the counter. "Good luck."

"Thanks, I need it." I grabbed a napkin and sat down at a table near a window overlooking Lighthouse Park.

Five minutes came and went. When it was twenty minutes past our arranged meeting time, I checked my e-mail. Nothing from the prospective babysitter. I logged onto BabySitNW.com and checked my account. I had the correct time. She'd stood me up. Well, cross that one off the list. The next person, a woman in her early twenties named Rachel, was due to arrive in fifteen minutes.

At our appointed meeting time, Rachel appeared in the doorway to the café. She looked exactly like her picture on the website. She searched the room and I waved. She smiled and came over to me.

"Hi." She extended her hand to me. "I'm Rachel."

"Nice to meet you, I'm Jill." I gestured for her to sit down.

"Do you mind if I get a cup of coffee first? I haven't had my caffeine yet for the day."

"Go ahead. This is my third cup." I took a big sip from it and smiled at her.

She bounced away with more energy than I'd ever had, even before having the kids. So far, so good. Rachel had been on time, seemed to have enough energy to play with Mikey, and she loved coffee. A girl after my own heart.

When she returned with her coffee, she sat down across from me and pulled out a notebook. I stared at her.

She noticed and said, "I like to be prepared and take notes so I don't forget things."

Check, check. Maybe this finding-a-babysitter thing wouldn't be as difficult as I'd imagined. It had started out rough, but things were improving. I went through my list of questions for her, including first-aid knowledge and work history. She passed them with flying colors. When I was through, I closed my notebook.

"I think you and my kids will be a good match. Do you have time to meet them this evening?"

"I'm sorry, I'm not available in the late afternoons and evenings. I'm taking nursing classes at the local community college." She looked apologetic. "It was in my profile."

My heart sunk. I really needed someone who was available in the evenings too in case I had to work a nighttime event at the Boathouse. I must have missed that detail about her availability when I was digging through all the babysitters on the site.

"Oh."

"But I'm available during the days." Her face was full of hope.

I couldn't say no. Rachel was my dream babysitter. Adam would be home most nights in the future, and we'd have to figure out how to make it work.

"How about we schedule a get-together for later in the week?"

"Sounds good." She smiled at me and pulled out her phone, ready to note our appointment on her calendar.

We arranged a meeting time, and we both stood. I shook her hand.

"I'm looking forward to meeting Mikey and Ella," she said.

"I'm sure they'll like you too."

She left the café, and Desi came over to my table.

"So did you find someone? You were talking to her for a while."

"I did. Unfortunately, she can't work evenings, but we'll work it out."

Desi nodded. "I'm glad you found someone. Now maybe you'll be less stressed."

"I doubt that." I looked through the window, past Lighthouse Park to the blue roof of the Boathouse. "Maybe when Declan's murderer is caught and we can put this behind us, I'll feel better about things."

"I'm sure that will be soon. I mentioned Lindsay's prenup to Tomàs, and he said he'd pass the information on. He also gave me another lecture about not getting involved. But how can I do that when I'm in a wedding with all of them?"

"I don't know." I bit my lip. "Maybe he's right."

"Oh, stop." Desi lifted her head and tilted it toward the counter. "I've got to help that customer, but stay for a few minutes longer if you can. I want to take a break, and I'd love some company."

She jetted off to help the new customer, and I pulled out my phone to check my calendar. It was jam-packed until after Labor Day. The achy feeling in my stomach returned, and I wondered if I had an ulcer. I pushed my coffee cup to the other side of the table.

The phone vibrated in my hands, startling me. Adam. "Hey, what's up? I'm so excited! I found someone to help with the kids. She's great."

He didn't say anything.

"What's wrong?" I immediately went into panic mode. "Is everything ok?"

"Yes, honey, everything is fine. It's just that I got roped into a last-minute business trip."

"When?"

He cleared his throat. "I fly out tonight. I'll be gone until Friday."

"But what about the kids? You were supposed to take care of Ella while I'm at work."

"I know, I'm sorry. I couldn't get out of this."

"You're supposed to be winding things down." I could hear the panic and whininess in my tone, but I couldn't help it.

"I am." His voice was harder. "Can't you take Ella with you to work? Mikey has school most of the day, so he shouldn't be a problem."

I didn't know what to say. It had been fine to take Ella when she was younger, but now it was difficult to keep her occupied for more than an hour or so in my office.

"I'll figure it out." I hung up the phone.

He immediately sent me a text.

I'm so sorry. I'll make it up to you. Love you.

My anger mellowed a little, but I needed to talk with someone before I let the feelings fester. Desi was slammed with customers on their morning coffee breaks, so I rang my mom.

"Hi, it's Jill."

"Hi, honey." Her voice took a more concerned tone. "Is something wrong?"

Motherly anxiety must be hereditary.

"Everyone's fine."

"Oh, good. You don't usually call during the middle of the day."

"I felt like talking and I had a break." I reached across the table for my coffee cup, forgetting about a possible ulcer, and wrapped my fingers around the smooth ceramic. The cup had grown cold, but talking with my mom warmed me.

"Hey, honey, I'm at the grocery store right now. Is it ok if I call you back in a little bit?"

"Sure, talk to you later." I sat at the table feeling very

alone. I'd had the good fortune to find a babysitter, but the specter of Declan's murder still hung over me like a dark cloud. I grabbed a discarded copy of the *Ericksville Times* from the table next to me. There was a huge picture of the Boathouse above the fold. I groaned. The article talked about how Declan's body had been found in the Sound, but he was actually killed at Lake Elinor. I checked the byline. Niely MacDonald strikes again.

I threw the paper down on the table next to me. I didn't have the emotional capacity to read the article. Something like this would only push the Boathouse further into the spotlight.

"I'm back." Desi plopped down in the chair opposite me with a large mug that contained a mocha with a healthy dose of chocolate syrup creating a rich brown swirl across the foam. "Whew. It's been busy today."

"That's good though." It hadn't been that long ago that Desi had gone full-time at the café. It was great to see the business so successful.

"So what's new with you?" She eyed me and took a big sip of the mocha, licking the chocolate off her lips when she was done.

"Adam just found out he's leaving on a business trip tonight. I don't know how I'm going to manage with both the kids and work." I propped my elbow on the table and leaned on it, cupping my chin. "The police still haven't discovered who killed Declan, and we got more cancellations today. I feel like I'm spending too much time trying to solve his murder and not enough time at the Boathouse. I should be doing damage control... or something to help."

"So you want to give up?" Desi raised her eyebrows. "I can't do this on my own, and we have to figure this out. I'm too close to everyone in the wedding party to be objective. I've been friends with most of them for over ten years."

"I don't know what else to do."

I didn't want to look at Desi, so I turned my attention to the walls where she had hung artwork from local artists. At the end of the wall, near the door, was an antique photograph of the Boathouse, probably taken when it was first built in the 1920s. The property had been in Desi and Adam's family that whole time. Beth and Lincoln had turned it into the premier event center that it was today and preserved that piece of family history. I couldn't let anything happen to it—the Boathouse was too important for my family's past and future.

I took a deep breath. "Ok. I'll give it another few days, but if we can't find anything out by the time all the guests leave Lake Elinor on Sunday, I'm done. Deal?"

She grinned. "Deal. I know we'll find something we can give to the police to help with their investigation. I can feel it."

"I hope you're right." For a moment, having a plan of attack lifted my spirits. Then, I remembered my childcare dilemma. "Adam has to go on a business trip tonight, so I have Ella at work with me for the rest of the week. Beth won't be back for at least another five days. What am I going to do?"

"I can help," Desi offered. "It hasn't been that busy here. My assistant can handle the café for a few days."

The bell over the door chimed and a group of elderly women in red hats walked in, lining up at the counter to order. Desi's assistant, Andrea, called out to her as she scurried around behind the counter, brewing the first beverage while taking the next order.

I eyed Desi. "I think there's your answer. You need to

take care of the café—it's your livelihood. I'll be fine until Beth gets back, ok?"

She regarded me dubiously. "Ok, but if things get sticky, I'm only a phone call away." She picked up her plate and mug, then walked briskly over to the counter.

I didn't have time to work myself into a tizzy about things because my mother called me back as soon as Desi left.

"Hey," I said then was quiet.

"What's wrong?" she asked. "You said everything was ok, but I can tell it's not."

I sighed. "Beth was visiting her sister in Portland and had some problems with her heart that landed her in the hospital."

"Oh, no," my mother said. "Is she ok?"

"She'll be fine, but she needed surgery, so she's stuck there for another several days. Adam was supposed to take care of the kids, but now he has to leave on a final business trip and can't do it. I hired a babysitter, but she can't start for a while and has a limited schedule, so I'll have Ella with me at work for a while. Everything is blowing up at the Boathouse, and I don't know what to do." I realized how whiny I sounded and cushioned my words. "But I'll figure it out, don't worry."

"You're not going to get much done with a nine-month-old hanging around. Do you want me to come out there? If I leave soon, I can get there by tonight."

"No, I don't want to impose on you. I'll figure it out."

"Honey, they are my grandchildren. It's not an imposition, and it's only a six-hour drive. I haven't seen them in almost two months, and I miss them. I'm happy to do it."

I stared out the window at the lighthouse. Was something finally going right?

"That would be great if you could come out here," I said with relief. Having my mom around to help would make a big difference in my stress levels.

"No problem. I'll see you tonight. I love you, honey."

"Love you too, Mom. See you soon."

She hung up and I pushed my chair back from the table, carrying my empty plate and mug over to the dish tub by the counter.

Having my mother bail me out was only a temporary solution and I didn't want to stress Beth out by asking her to help watch the kids when she returned, so I had to figure our childcare situation out ASAP. If I could get that done and miraculously figure out who'd killed Declan, maybe life could get back to normal.

16

I awoke the next morning to the aroma of bacon and eggs. I passed by the kids' rooms, but judging by all the noise downstairs, they were already awake.

"Hi, Mommy," Mikey called out in a sing-song voice. "Did you know Grandma was here?" Without waiting for a response, he said, "I'm showing her how I can do forward rolls like we learned in gymnastics at school." He pitched himself across the carpeted living room floor in an awkward imitation of a somersault.

My mother clapped and winked at me from where she was setting breakfast on the dining table. "He's getting to be quite a good gymnast."

Mikey puffed up and said solemnly, "I'm almost ready for the Olympics."

I laughed. "Maybe in a few more years." I directed him over to his seat. "This smells delicious. Can I help with anything?" She'd been busy this morning. Along with the bacon and eggs, she'd cut up a cantaloupe, and filled a bowl with strawberries and blueberries. She'd arrived last night after the kids were in bed, and we'd gone over my schedule for the next few days to confirm who would pick up Mikey at school each day.

"Nope, we're good. Sit down and eat before you have to leave." She placed a mug of coffee in front of me on the table. I smiled gratefully and drank it as quickly as I could without burning my tongue. After finishing breakfast, I showered and dressed, then said goodbye to everyone. Mikey was so excited to have his grandmother around that he didn't even seem to care that I was leaving.

I had a routine doctor's appointment for myself in Seattle that morning, so to make good on my promise to Desi, I made up an excuse to drive a few more miles from my doctor's office to visit Jared at the dental office he operated with Bill and Declan. Mine was the first car in the parking lot, so I waited to see if he'd come in to work that day. I figured with Declan gone and Bill out for wedding preparations that week, he probably had more than a few patients to see.

When he arrived, I got out of my car.

"Hi," I said, waving to him as he opened his car door.

He cocked his head to the side. "Hi. Not that I'm not happy to see you, but what are you doing here? Did we have an appointment?"

"Sorry to show up like this, but I was hoping I could chat with you for a few minutes about your audio–visual needs for the best man's speech."

"Ok." He looked puzzled. "Wouldn't it have been easier to do this over the phone? I feel bad that you came down here."

"Oh, no. It was no problem. I had a doctor's appointment downtown, and I thought I'd swing by here and see you in person." I made a show of looking at the building. "This is such a nice office building. And those flowers..." I swept my hands in front of me, over the manicured beds of rhododendrons and various perennials. They really were gorgeous and had a wonderful aroma. I sniffed deeply. "They're so beautiful."

He seemed perplexed by my babbling, but at least it had taken his mind off my flimsy excuse to visit him. He got out of the car holding a laptop bag and a cup of coffee. A small ticket had attached itself to his foot, and it fell off in the parking lot.

"Oh, you dropped something!" I dipped down to pick it up and held it out to him. Before he grabbed it, my eyes honed in on the text on the paper. It was a race slip from Azure Downs, the local horse-racing track, dated the same day as the rehearsal dinner.

He ripped it from my hand. "Thanks. Now, what did you need to talk with me about?"

"Your audio–visual needs for your speech at the wedding," I reminded him.

"Oh yeah. I'm planning on doing a video with music and playing it from my laptop. Do you have a projector and screen?"

"We do." I smiled at him. "That's no problem, but I'm glad I asked. It can take a while for our crew to set it up."

"Great, great." He moved toward the door.

Before he could go in, I asked, "I noticed you arguing with Lindsay the other day. I'm not sure why, but she seems to have taken a dislike to me. Is there something bothering her, other than Declan's death?"

He scowled. "Lindsay is always after money. She wanted

me to liquidate Declan's share of the practice as soon as possible. I told her that wouldn't be happening." He kicked a small pebble off the sidewalk. "His share wouldn't be worth much anyway. The business hasn't been doing well."

"Oh. I'm sorry to hear that. This must be such a stressful time for all of you." I glanced at his car. "I'm glad you got your car back though. It's lucky they were able to fix it."

"What? Oh, yes. I got it back last Friday. The BMW dealership is wonderful. They even delivered my car to me as part of their service."

"Wow, that is great." I highly doubted the local mechanics would be that generous the next time my minivan was in the shop.

He jerked his hand at the door. "I have patients to see soon, and I need to get things set up. Is there anything else you need from me?"

"Nope, have a great day. I'll see you at the wedding on Saturday." I gave him my most winning smile.

He waved and entered the building.

On the way back to the Boathouse, I thought about what he'd said. This was the second time that I'd heard that the dental practice was having financial difficulties. Becca didn't seem to think that was true though. Had Bill kept it from her? He prided himself on being completely honest, so unless that was all a ruse, he wasn't aware of any financial issues. Could Declan have been involved with something shady with the business? Was that what had gotten him killed?

After my preschool volunteer shift was over, I stopped at the BeansTalk for a quick pick-me-up. To my surprise, Becca was in there chatting with Desi at a corner table. Desi's assistant served me my coffee and donut in a bag, and I waved at Desi. They looked like they were deep in conversation, and I didn't want to disturb them.

To my surprise, Becca waved me over. I joined them at their table, and Desi motioned for me to sit down.

"Sit. We were just discussing some bridesmaid stuff."

I shrugged. "I have a few minutes before I need to be at work."

"Did you get the catering order updated?" Becca asked.

"I did." I munched on my donut. "It's all taken care of."

"That's a relief." Becca picked at the muffin on her plate. "At least one thing is going right."

Desi looked at her. "What's wrong?"

Becca hesitated and then her face crumpled. "It's Lindsay."

"Ah." I waited for her to continue.

She pulled a tissue out of her purse and dabbed her eyes. "She knows something about me, and she's threatening to tell Bill."

"What is it?" Desi asked.

"It's too embarrassing." She pushed the plate away.

"You can tell us. We won't tell anyone. It'll do you good to get it off your chest." Desi patted her on the arm. "It's not healthy for you to be so stressed before your wedding."

Becca's face flushed. "A few years ago, Bill and I broke up for a couple of months. It was over something stupid, and we eventually realized that. But, while we were apart, I had a one-night stand with Jared."

Desi's eyes widened. "Jared?"

Becca nodded. "Unfortunately. It was so stupid. I'd had too much to drink, and I was mad at Bill." She looked miserable.

"Oh, Becca." Desi's lips turned down. "Why is Lindsay doing this? It's not like you cheated on Bill. He'll understand."

"She wants me to keep something from the police." She scanned the room. "I saw her and Declan fighting down by his boat the night he died. She said if I report her, she'll tell Bill about Jared." She gave us a pleading look. "I don't want him to find out two days before our wedding. It'll hurt him too much."

"You have to tell the police," Desi said. "What if Lindsay was the one who killed Declan?"

"I don't know if I can do it." Becca twisted her napkin into a spiral.

"Becs, I'm sorry, but I have to tell Tomàs if you won't. I can't keep this from him. It could be important to the murder investigation, and he'd never forgive me if I kept something like that a secret."

"Do you really think she could have murdered her own husband?" Becca's eyes shifted between Desi and I.

"I don't know." Desi's shoulders slumped. "I wouldn't have thought so."

Becca spoke softly. "I heard a truck out there, that night. Bill was next to me in bed, so I know it wasn't him, but do you think it could have been Lindsay moving Declan's boat? I mean, she must have known how to trailer it with all the time Declan spent out on the water."

"You have to tell the police about that too," I urged. "If nothing else, it gives Bill an alibi."

"Ok, but can you give me until tonight to call the police? I want to tell Bill first, before Lindsay tells him anything."

Desi contemplated that. Finally, she said, "All right. But you need to tell the police before tomorrow morning, ok?"

"Ok, I'll do it." She took a deep breath then smiled tentatively at Desi. "Hey, did I tell you I was offered a tenure-track position in California?"

Desi shook her head no. "That's so exciting. It's what you've always wanted. Are you going to take it?"

"No, Bill has his practice here. But it's great to have been considered."

"But you've always wanted this. What did he say when you told him?"

"I didn't tell him." Becca fidgeted in her seat. "I still feel guilty about that night with Jared. I know I didn't technically cheat on Bill, but it sure feels like it."

"You need to tell him," Desi said gently. "He'll understand. And I think he'd like to know about the job opportunity. That's big news."

I was beginning to wish I hadn't been present for this conversation. I wasn't close to Becca like Desi was, and I felt like I was intruding. However, we had learned something new about the night Declan died. If only it would lead to the murderer being caught.

"Girls, I have to get going. Thanks for inviting me to sit with you." I waved then hurried over to the Boathouse. If I was going to make Becca's wedding perfect like I'd promised her, I had a lot of work to do.

17

"*A*re you sure you have to go out to Lake Elinor?" Worry clouded my mother's face as she rocked Ella in her arms. "It could be dangerous. Didn't you say one of the people staying at that house probably murdered their friend?"

When I heard it that way, it didn't sound terribly smart, but I'd already made the commitment. Besides, I was meeting Bill and I didn't think he was the killer.

"It will be fine. I'm meeting the groom there. Nothing is going to happen to me in broad daylight." I peered at her face. My words had done little to assure her. "I already screwed up their rehearsal dinner, so I have to do whatever I can to salvage the Boathouse's reputation. If that means having to make house calls for their every whim, I'll do it."

She sighed and kissed Ella's head. "Ok, but call me when you leave. I want to know you're ok."

"Yes, Mom." I grinned. She still treated me like I was a teenager sometimes, but I knew she loved me. I'd enjoyed having her come for a visit, especially to have some adult company in the house. However, I'd studiously avoided asking her anything about her separation from my father. Time would tell how that would turn out. Goldie nudged my feet and gave me a begging look.

"Oh, all right, you can come with me today." I hadn't been spending as much time with him as I used to since starting work at the Boathouse. It would do him good to run around a little at Lake Elinor. Not in the pristine house, of course. Becca's tiny Chihuahua was more suited to that than my rowdy golden retriever. I didn't see any harm in letting him out on a leash in the yard or the dock, but I'd ask Bill to make sure it was all right.

When I got to the lake, Bill told me to bring Goldie inside.

"Are you sure?" Goldie wasn't muddy, but he also wasn't predictable and I didn't know how he'd handle being around their Chihuahua.

"Yeah, I'm sure." He laughed. "We have Tilly and my future in-laws have a Saint Bernard. It may not look like it, but this house is pretty dog-proof."

I looked around. "Where is Tilly?"

"She's locked up in the bedroom. She sometimes gets agitated by strange men, and I didn't want her to get upset by the repairman who's coming."

I shrugged. "Ok then." I followed him into the house with Goldie in tow, who insisted on sniffing every inch of the entry hall.

"Thanks for coming all the way out here," Bill said as he led me toward the back of the house to the study. "Becca arranged for someone to come and fix the oven. When we tried to cook a lasagna yesterday, it wouldn't turn on. We ended up ordering a pepperoni pizza from the local pizzeria. It seems like nothing is going quite like we expected this week." He opened the door for Goldie to go out on the enclosed deck. Goldie took off immediately to stick his nose through the slats in the railing.

"No problem. I don't mind. I want to make sure everything is perfect for your wedding." I looked around the study. "What did you want to go over with me?"

"I was hoping I could go over the final costs one more time, given the changes Becca made. And I can pay you today." He shook his head. "With everything that's happened, I'd like to be able to enjoy our wedding and honeymoon as much as possible and not be worrying about paying then."

"Oh, well, thanks." If I'd known that reviewing the final costs and giving me a check was all he wanted me to come out here for, I could've e-mailed the invoice and had them mail us a check. However, I needed to make sure that everything went smoothly with this event, so I didn't mind going the extra mile.

"Do you have the final invoice for me? I know Becca had made some changes to our catering." He smiled at me. "I know she can be a little demanding sometimes, but she has very definite ideas about what she wants. Thanks for being so great about working with us."

I handed him the invoice I'd printed out before I left the Boathouse. "It's been a joy working with both of you. Here's your invoice. I've added in the cost for the change to the entrées that Becca made."

He scanned the piece of paper. "This charge doesn't look quite right." He poked his finger at one of the lines. I leaned in closer to see what it was.

"Oh, that's the charge for the table linens and settings."

"Shouldn't it be a little higher?" asked Bill. "It looks about the same as it was before we added all of those people on. I would have thought we'd need to increase the number of tables."

I flushed. He was right. Although I had informed the catering staff that we needed entrées for all of the extra guests that Becca had added on this week, I hadn't changed the other charges on their invoice.

"You know, you're right. Thank you for saying something. Let me just update that for you." I pulled out my cell phone and turned on the calculator app. After a minute of jotting down figures, I tabulated the results and gave him the final number.

"It's about what I was expecting. Let me get my checkbook." Bill pulled the checkbook out from the center drawer of the desk. He neatly wrote out the check and signed it, then recorded it in his check register and handed it to me.

The house was quiet, and I hadn't noticed many cars outside.

"Is anyone else here today?" Perhaps my mother didn't have anything to worry about if only Bill was here. After all, Becca's statement about the mystery truck driver had exonerated him.

"Becca left to get her nails done for the wedding." He smiled softly. "You know girls, trying to turn themselves into princesses for the wedding. Although with Becca, it doesn't take very much."

"Desi mentioned that the two of you met while you were in college. Have you been together since then?

"We dated for a few years and then broke up for a couple of months." He frowned. "Those were the worst few months of my life. I realized after only a day that I'd taken her for granted. I'm so lucky to have her in my life. She's so smart, and she works so hard at her job. I'm really proud of her." He beamed at me.

"She does seem special," I agreed, then looked out the window to the deck, which was empty. "Where is everybody else?"

I tried to act nonchalant, but I think part of me wanted to make sure there wasn't a murderer hiding behind the next door.

"Orson is here somewhere, but he's generally so quiet that I don't even hear him most of the time. I'm not sure about Jared." He laughed. "I don't think Jared will ever settle down. Given the chance, he'd be out at the bars every night, partying away into the early hours of the morning." He shook his head. "I don't know how he manages to get to work in the morning looking so bright and chipper. I went with him to the casino last Wednesday after the rehearsal dinner to blow off a little steam. With Declan and Lindsay fighting, we were both pretty stressed out."

"Oh, which casino did you go to?"

"The one out by Islington."

"That's the new one, right? I've never been there." With two kids at home, I didn't get out much and wasn't much of a gambler anyway, although I did have dreams of going to Las Vegas with Adam for a couples vacation and maybe even taking in a few shows. However, the casinos in the area were well known for their all-you-can-eat buffets, which Beth and Lincoln loved, so I'd been to quite a few of them for dinner.

"Yes, it is. Jared was itching to try it out. Apparently it's the only casino in the area he hadn't been to." Bill seemed a little perturbed by his own statement.

"He sounds like my mother-in-law. She loves trying out the slot machines at all of the casinos in the area. She doesn't gamble too much and sticks with the penny machines, but she has a ton of fun." I remembered the racetrack slip in Jared's car and had a sneaking suspicion that he didn't stick to the penny machines.

"I didn't try the slot machines. I played a little roulette but soon grew bored. Jared was playing blackjack and I couldn't drag him away from the tables, so I nursed a beer in the bar for an hour. I finally had to tell Jared that we were leaving." He shook his head again. "If he hadn't gotten a ride with me because his car was in the shop, I don't know if we would've seen him until morning. He's living quite the bachelor's lifestyle. But he's not always like that. I think he just likes blackjack."

He seemed envious of his friend's lifestyle to some extent, and I didn't think that he had any idea that Jared might be more than a casual gambler.

"So Declan didn't go with the two of you to the casino that night?"

"No, I never saw him after he stalked out of our rehearsal dinner. I tried to catch him, but he slipped away from me."

"Do you think something had been bothering him? I mean, I don't know him or Lindsay very well, but they seemed to go from zero to sixty in no time. Did he normally blow up like that?"

"No, Declan's always had somewhat of a temper, but he'd been really secretive lately." He thought about it for a moment. "But Lindsay could really push his buttons. She'd had her lawyer request a valuation of our dental practice. Declan had started the valuation process with an expert at the CPA firm we use."

"Was he thinking of selling his share in the practice?"

Bill shifted on his feet and stared out the window, then sighed. "I don't know if he would have gone through with it. He told me not to tell Jared because he wasn't sure what he was going to do, and he didn't want to upset him. I guess I can tell Jared now. I've hated having to keep it a secret from him."

"Was Lindsay trying to get his share in the divorce?" I leaned against the wall, tapping the check against my fingertips.

"I don't know what Lindsay was trying to do. I never knew what she wanted." He cleared his throat. "Anyway, I really shouldn't be talking about her. She's gone through a lot in this last week, and I know Becca is worried about her."

"Yes, she has gone through a lot. It's awful. I can't imagine losing my husband like that." I smiled sympathetically at him.

The doorbell rang, and Bill seemed to realize that he was telling me his friend's secrets.

"I better get that. It's probably the oven repair guy." He motioned to the check. "I don't think there was anything else that I needed to discuss with you—did you have anything for me?"

"Nope, I think that's it," I said brightly. "Thanks for this. I'll see you on Saturday." I grabbed Goldie off the deck and brushed past the oven repair man, shutting the door behind me on the way out. Before I could reach my car, someone called out my name. I turned to see who it was.

"Orson, hi." I walked across the grass to the lower deck, where he was sitting in a patio chair gazing out at the lake.

"Pull up a chair." He gestured at a chair a few feet away.

I'd been meaning to speak with Orson, and I was already out at Lake Elinor, so this seemed as good a chance as any. I reached for the chair and dragged it closer to him, wincing at the noise as it trailed along the wooden boards. This deck level was also fully enclosed, so I let Goldie off his leash to roam freely.

"Are you the only one here besides Bill?" From Bill, I knew the answer to that question, but I wanted to see what Orson said.

"Yes, it's quite relaxing without everyone else here."

"It seems like there's a bit of drama going on in the house," I observed.

He sighed. "Unfortunately, there is. After Declan died, I thought some of Lindsay's hostility would dissipate, but it seems that she's shifted her anger to Jared instead. But she's been through a lot this week."

I noticed that he'd echoed Bill's statement regarding Lindsay. The last couple times I'd been here, Orson had appeared to cater to Lindsay's needs, and I wondered if there was romantic involvement between them.

Evidently, I'd asked that question out loud.

"No, Lindsay and I have never dated. She's been with Declan since the first time I met her." He frowned. "She hasn't appeared very happy in the last few years though. I think their relationship was taking a toll on her. I've tried to be there for her, but she keeps pushing me away." He gazed wistfully out over the lake.

It appeared my suspicions had been correct. He did have feelings for Lindsay, although they didn't seem to be reciprocated. A thought struck me. While he'd been looking out for Lindsay, had he seen her arguing with Declan down on the boat dock at Lake Elinor on the night Declan died?

"Did you see the fight that she had with Declan last Wednesday night?" I carefully examined his face.

"You mean the one that she had with him at the rehearsal dinner? Yeah, everyone saw that."

"No, I mean after the rehearsal dinner, when both of them came back to the house. I heard that the two of them had a big argument down on the boat dock."

"Oh, that." His eyes met mine and his tone became weary. "Do the police know about that too?"

I honestly wasn't sure. Becca was supposed to have told the police about the quarrels she'd witnessed between Lindsay and Declan that night, but Desi hadn't confirmed with me that she had.

"I don't think so, not yet." I put my hand on the deck railing, rubbing my palm across the smooth, splinter-free wood.

"She didn't kill him."

"How do you know that?" I leaned against the railing, not taking my eyes off of him.

He shifted uneasily in his patio chair. "I was watching the two of them out there to make sure she was ok. I saw her come in, and she didn't leave after that. Declan was still out there, downing beers like there was no tomorrow." He reddened. "I'm sorry. That was a poor choice of words."

I turned the information around in my mind. He'd confirmed what Becca had told us about Lindsay and Declan's second fight of the night. But then how had Declan gone from drinking like a fish to swimming with the fishes?

"And Jared and Bill were out of the house until pretty late at night, right?"

"They were. I heard them come in around one in the morning. They wouldn't have seen Declan because I'd looked out the window about midnight, and he was already gone." His eyes widened. "What if the police were wrong about him being murdered? He might have fallen off the dock and hit his head on his boat. I saw him leaning against it and then staggering back onto the dock when it shifted in the water." Panic tinged his voice. "What if he was still alive after he fell in? I should have gone out there to check on him. I've been boating since I was a kid. I know better than to allow someone in that condition to be around the water. But I didn't want to let him know I'd been watching them."

His fawning over Lindsay had been annoying, but now I felt bad for the guy. "I don't think he fell in." Or if he had, someone had at the very least moved his body from the lake to the Sound. "Someone had a hand in his death. I doubt there was anything you could have done."

"I guess." He slumped back in the chair.

Goldie barked loudly. A robin had landed on the railing, just out of his reach. I attached the leash to his collar before he could make another attempt. The sun was high overhead, and I'd been out at Lake Elinor for far longer than I'd anticipated.

"I'd better get back to the Boathouse. If I want to meet Becca's wedding expectations, I've got a lot to take care of before tomorrow."

"Right, right, of course. Well, have a nice afternoon. I think I'm going to see about some lunch." He wandered off toward the back of the deck, where a door led into the house.

I left the house more confused than ever. Bill didn't seem to have any awareness of financial issues with the practice, if there even were any. Orson claimed Lindsay had been safely in the house and had nothing to do with her husband's death. Jared and Bill had been out at the casino when Declan disappeared. Something wasn't adding up here. I called my mom to let her know I was safe and drove home.

18

The bridal party was due to arrive at the Boathouse at ten for the preparations preceding the three o'clock wedding. Becca had a tight schedule involving makeup, hair styling, and wedding photos prior to the ceremony.

Desi walked in, carrying her lavender bridesmaid's dress in a plastic garment bag over her arm.

"Hey." She hugged me with her free arm. "Am I ever glad to see you."

"Why, what's up?"

"I had to go with Becca down to the police station last night to tell them about Lindsay and Declan fighting on the dock at Lake Elinor the night he was killed." She scrunched up her face. "It wasn't a fun experience. I'm normally there as the wife bringing her husband his lunch. This time, I felt like I was part of the investigation, and not in a good way." She shivered and hugged her arms to her chest. "It brought back way too many bad memories of when Mr. Westen was killed."

"What do you mean?" I beckoned her down the hallway to the privacy of my office.

"They treated us like we were suspects, not witnesses." She sat down in the chair opposite my ergonomic swivel chair with the dress resting carefully on her lap.

"Well, Becca was at the house the night Declan was killed." Come to think of it, no one I'd talked to had mentioned her whereabouts that night. I'd only had her word that she was in bed when Declan disappeared.

"Yeah, but I'm sure she didn't do it. She doesn't have it in her. Besides, what reason would she have to kill him?"

"True." I shut my office door to keep anyone from over-hearing. "Did she tell Bill about her relationship with Jared?"

"I think so," Desi said. "At least she told me she was going to."

"Yikes. I wonder how that will go over right before the wedding."

"It was the right thing to do though. A secret like that could tear a marriage apart."

I nodded. "Have you seen her or Bill yet?"

"No." Desi stood. "I'd better get in there. They're in the Puget Room, right?"

"Yes. You're the first to arrive though." We usually rented the smaller Puget Room along with the main hall of the Boathouse for weddings so the bride had somewhere to get ready and for everyone in the wedding party to have a place to store their belongings.

I opened the door. Sounds of laughter came down the hallway.

Becca and Bill were alone in the lobby holding hands, with big smiles on their faces. Desi and I exchanged glances.

"It doesn't look like she told him." I peeked around the corner again. Still bubbly, happy, soon-to-be newlyweds, like most other couples on their wedding day.

"Maybe she told him, and he didn't care? Bill really is a nice guy." She tipped her head toward where the wedding party was gathering. "I'd better get over to the Puget Room though. I think Becca has me early on the list for the makeup artist."

"Ooh. Sounds fun. You'll look gorgeous with professional makeup." I was a little jealous. Maybe after the summer rush was over, Adam and I could splurge on a fancy dinner and I could get a mini makeover beforehand.

Desi strode off down the hall toward Becca and Bill. They parted when they saw her, then they all disappeared around the corner in the direction of the Puget Room.

Lindsay came in through the front door, fighting with her dress bag and several duffel bags of what I presumed to be wedding essentials.

"Here, let me help you." I pasted a smile on my face.

She shoved all of the duffel bags at me. I stumbled back a little under the weight, and she breezed off without a second glance back at me. One of things I was most looking forward to about this wedding being over was to never have to see Lindsay Becker ever again. Becca's mom and her cousin Isabel had arrived, and along with Desi, were getting the room situated for the day's events. In the minute it took me to walk down the hall hefting the bags, Lindsay had already poured herself a glass of champagne and was downing it faster than advisable.

Bill wasn't in the room—he must have gone into the Snowton Room, a tiny room at the end of the hallway that the grooms used. It was big enough for two couches and a flat screen TV and that was about it, but we'd never received any complaints from grooms.

I deposited Lindsay's bag next to the couch. "I'll be in my office for most of the day. Please don't hesitate to ask if you need anything."

Becca smiled. "Thanks, Jill. Thanks for everything. I peeked into the main hall, and the decorations are really coming along. It's going to look just as magical as I've always imagined."

Her mother walked up to her and hugged her, looking like she was going to cry. "I can't believe my baby is getting married."

"Mom, I'm thirty-two and I've been with Bill for over ten of those years. It's time," she joked. "Don't cry." A few tears slipped out of her own eyes.

Desi plucked a Kleenex from the box we kept on an end table and handed it to her. Weddings tended to be teary events, and we usually went through at least one box in the bride's room with every wedding.

I eased out of the room and retreated toward my office, first checking on the progress in the main hall. Becca was right. The wedding preparations were on track.

"Nice job, everything looks great," I called out to the staff. "I'll be in my office if you need me." They turned, surprised to see someone else there, then gave me a thumbs-up and returned to work.

I kept my door ajar in case anyone needed me, but otherwise was head down on planning for my next event. Around lunchtime, someone knocked on my door, but to my surprise, it wasn't anyone involved with Becca and Bill's wedding.

"Hi, honey," my mother said, holding Ella in her arms. Mikey peeked around her into my office.

"Hi." I came around my desk to give Mikey a hug. "I didn't expect to see you here today."

"Oh, I hope I'm not intruding, but we wanted to drop off some lunch for you." She handed me a thermal bag. I rifled through it, discovering an egg salad sandwich, potato chips, and some carrots.

"Thanks. I love egg salad." I gave her a quick hug and kissed Ella's head. A thought occurred to me. "Hey, do you want to see the event I'm working on in progress?"

A wide smile crossed her face. "I'd love that. I've never been able to visit you at work before."

I led her down the hallway toward the main room. "We're hosting a wedding tonight. Actually, it's the wedding for Desi's friends." I waved my arm across the vast room. "See, they're setting up the chairs for the ceremony now."

"Cool," Mikey said. I caught him right before he took off down the aisle to terrorize the perfectly straight rows of chairs.

"It's lovely." My mother bounced Ella in her arms. "And you're in charge of this event?"

"Yes. Beth was supposed to manage it, but since she's in Portland, I took over." I gazed at the room, taking it in through her eyes. It would be a gorgeous wedding, with the white chairs and a rose-covered arbor at the front. The sliding barn doors were open, allowing the sun to shine in and the fresh air off Puget Sound to fill the room.

"You should be proud of yourself. This took a lot of work."

"Well, I had a little help." Still, my mother's words of praise meant a lot to me. Taking over for Beth hadn't been easy, but I thought I'd done quite well.

She gave the scene another once-over and smiled at me. "We'd better get going. I'm taking Mikey to the park."

"Yeah!" Mikey grabbed her hand and tried to lead her out of the room. She allowed him to pull her toward the door, and gave me a little wave before departing.

I returned to my office feeling certain that the wedding would be a success.

Miracle of miracles, the wedding ceremony went off without a hitch—even having Tilly the Chihuahua as a ring bearer. Lindsay had stayed sober long enough to perform her duties as bridesmaid, and Becca looked lovely. Bill had enlisted his cousin to take Declan's place as a groomsman.

The wedding party exited, and while Becca and Bill positioned themselves against a wall near the exit doors, Lindsay made a beeline for the open bar we'd set up in the lobby. Apparently she intended to rectify her sober state as quickly as possible.

They'd rented out the entire Boathouse for their wedding, and while the guests went through the receiving line and milled around the lobby, the staff were quickly moving the white wooden chairs around the round tables to prepare for dinner to be served.

When the dinner configuration was set up, Bill and Becca led the group into the room and seated themselves at the small table up on the raised stage. After everyone was seated, the catering staff served the entreés as I watched from a corner of the main room. I'd remembered to make sure that Becca's feuding cousins were separated, and everything was going like clockwork. Until the speeches.

Desi stood to give her speech as matron of honor, looking beautiful in her lavender bridesmaid dress. Her face had been made-up expertly and her hair styled in a sweeping updo. Tomàs couldn't take his eyes off her throughout the speech. They'd been married for many years, had two small children, and had endured trials in their marriage, including Desi being suspected of murder, yet they were still deeply in love. If I were giving a speech, they'd be the perfect example of what Becca and Bill should aspire to. I really hoped Becca had told Bill her secret.

As Desi wound down her speech and the audience started clapping, Lindsay stumbled to her feet, reminding me that Becca had told her she could give the first speech. Had she changed her mind?

Lindsay shouted, "My turn. I want to tell them what marriage is really like."

Orson tried to pull her back to her seat, but Lindsay couldn't be dissuaded. She pushed him away again and again.

"Want to know what marriage is really like? I'll tell you. It starts out nice and lovey-dovey, like these two." She used the microphone to point to the newly married couple. Tears started to slur her words past what the alcohol had already done. "But then a few years go by, and your husband decides you aren't young enough or pretty enough. And it all goes down the drain. That's what marriage is. A big fat lie." She dropped the microphone on the floor and ran out of the room, sobbing. Orson grabbed her purse and chased after her.

Up on the stage, Becca had her mouth open in horror, and a pained expression filled Bill's face.

Jared grabbed the microphone. "Well, that was an interesting perspective on marriage. Luckily, these two were meant for each other." He smiled at the stage. "They've got a lifetime of happiness in front of them." He raised his glass of champagne and toasted them.

Becca and Bill kissed and the crowd cheered. Jared handed the microphone to Isabel, who began a long-winded speech about how she'd first heard Becca talking about Bill. I slipped out of the room to check on the cake and to make sure Tilly was still doing ok in the storage room I'd put her in until the end of the reception.

The tall, white, multi-tiered cake embellished with silver balls and icing was perched on a bed of white lace on top of a rolling table, ready to go. I checked in with the staff, and they were on the ball with the other details.

I continued monitoring the festivities as the night wore on. The DJ had the crowd pumped up and everyone was dancing and laughing, just what we wanted to see at a wedding. I pushed open the door to the outside deck. The air was fresh and cool coming off the Sound. Cheers came through the closed doors leading out of the main hall, bouncing off the water.

Becca and Bill were scheduled to jet off to their honeymoon cabin on Willowby Island via Declan's boat, so I wanted to make sure it was ready to go for their departure. The police had released the boat from evidence in time for the wedding. It seemed fitting that their good friend's boat would be used to take them to the start of their new life together—almost like he was with them on their wedding day. The sun was setting, a gorgeous collage of pinks, purples, and oranges that streaked the sky over the island. A perfect, romantic night fit for newlyweds.

The gate was open to the docks, much like it had been the morning I found Declan's body. My mood turned from contemplative elation to a sense of dread. We always kept the gate closed, with a child-proof lock on it, just in case there were any pint-sized escapees from an event. I forced myself to walk toward it. *It's silly to worry, Jill. Someone prob-*

ably put wedding bells or tin cans on the boat and forgot to close it behind themselves.

My trepidation continued until I was at the top of the ramp leading down to the boat docks. A woman with blonde hair lay in a puddle of lavender silk on the wood planks in front of Declan's boat.

"Lindsay!" I ran down the ramp as fast as I dared and stood in front of her. The body didn't move. My heart beat faster. "Lindsay," I said again, crouching down to nudge her shoulder with my hand. She stirred and I plopped backwards, looking up at the sky. *Thank goodness.* I helped her sit up.

"Where am I?" She looked at me groggily. Clumps of mascara dotted her face, and strands of hair had come loose from the bobby-pinned coif on the top of her head.

"You're on the docks in front of the Boathouse, at Becca's wedding," I said helpfully.

She stared up at the blue-roofed boathouse, then back to Declan's boat and groaned. "Why am I down here?"

"I couldn't tell you. You disappeared with Orson right after your speech." I looked around. There weren't many places to hide on the small floating docks. "Where's Orson?"

"My speech." She closed her eyes and then opened them. They were bright with fresh tears. "I ruined Becca's wedding."

I handed her a Kleenex out of the emergency pack I carried with me at all times during an event. She dabbed at her face.

"I don't know where Orson went." Lindsay stared into space. "He followed me out to the deck, but after I told him there was never going to be anything between the two of us, he stormed off." She looked down at the dock, tracing a knot in the wood with her fingers. "I think I really hurt his feelings." She drew her knees up to her chest, the lavender silk catching and snagging on the rough boards. "I've screwed up everything."

"No, no. I'm sure you haven't," I said in a lame attempt to console her. She continued to sob, and I handed her another Kleenex.

She honked her nose in a most un-ladylike fashion and then stared with dull eyes at Declan's boat.

"He loved this boat. It was the first thing he bought when the practice started to turn a profit. He used to take it out fishing on the Sound with Bill, Jared, and Orson. It was one of his favorite things to do." She reached out to touch the smooth sides of the boat. "I could never be out there for long. I get seasick as soon as I step on a boat." Her face had taken on a green cast, and she covered her mouth. "I don't think this floating dock is much better."

She got to her feet in record time and leaned over the deck to throw up. Out of my bag came another rescue Kleenex.

"Thanks," she said, wiping around her mouth. She turned to walk up the ramp, holding tightly to the aluminum railing as she climbed the metal treads. I followed behind her, closing the gate behind us. She threw the used tissues in the trash container on the deck then leaned over the railing, breathing deeply. "I love it out here. I wish I could go out on the water. Maybe my marriage wouldn't have fallen apart if I could have shared in Declan's passion for boating."

I stood near her and patted her back. "I'm sure he knew you would have if you could."

Her eyes took a far-off look. "We had so many good

times together, but he could make me so angry." Her face reddened. "And then when he asked for the divorce, I knew it was over."

"When was the last time you saw him?"

"That night at Lake Elinor. We talked down by the dock there. That one didn't float like this one." She looked pointedly down at our floating docks. "He was talking about taking out the boat on the lake, but he was too drunk. I told him not to, but eventually I gave up and went back in the house."

Lindsay's rendition fit with Orson's, that she'd come in to the house, leaving Declan alone on the docks. I still didn't know what had happened after that. Had he taken his boat out on the lake and drowned somehow? How had his boat ended up here, tied up at the Boathouse docks the next morning, with his body floating next to it? None of this made sense, but I felt like I was getting closer to the truth.

My watch read nine o'clock. "Lindsay, you should get back in there. They'll be cutting the cake soon. If you feel up to it, I'm sure Becca would be happy to have you there."

She nodded. "I think I'm ok now. No more champagne tonight though."

She still looked a little green around the gills but seemed to be able to walk in a straight line. I walked into the Boathouse with her, making sure she got in there ok. I didn't want someone else dying on my watch.

Lindsay had said that Declan's boat was there that night, at Lake Elinor. He could have hit his head, fallen in the water, and drowned. Could the coroner have been wrong? Was Lindsay telling the truth, or had someone taken Declan's body and dumped it in Puget Sound to divert attention from themselves? At the front of the room, Becca and Bill were cutting the cake and smashing it into each other's faces while chortling. Their guests clapped and smiled broadly. With all the happiness emanating throughout the room, it was hard to believe that someone there had killed a friend the week before, leaving his body just outside the room they now occupied.

19

I sidled up to Desi while Becca threw the bouquet. "Did she say if she told Bill?" I whispered.

Desi smiled. "She told him. I guess he was upset, but then he calmed down and was glad she told him. He'd been worried about whatever was bothering her."

"Good. It seemed to be eating at her to keep that from him." I glanced at Becca. "She looks so happy."

"You did a great job on their wedding." She patted me on the back. "They told me they were thrilled with how it turned out."

"Thanks." I thought it had gone well, but it was nice to hear it from someone else. "You know, I talked to Lindsay out on the docks."

Her eyebrows shot up. "Out on the docks? Why was she out there?"

"I think she was mourning the loss of Declan. She was really upset, and surprisingly nice to me. I think this has all affected her more than you'd think."

"I agree. With the impending divorce and then the loss of her soon-to-be ex, there has to be a lot running through her head. She didn't use to be so, um..." Desi paused, searching for the right word.

"Ornery?" I finished, laughing.

"Right."

The crowd parted and the barn-style doors at the back of the main room were opened to allow access to the docks. Becca and Bill walked hand-in-hand down the aisle and out through the doors. Jared handed Bill the boat key, and the crowd cheered when he held it up in the air. The bride and groom walked down the ramp to Declan's boat, which they were using as a getaway vehicle. Lindsay and Isabel brought their bags to them, and they tossed them into the back of the uncovered boat and climbed in. Everyone, including Desi and I, waved goodbye as they sped away into the night, the running lights tracing their path as they skimmed across the waves.

Lindsay made a beeline for the stairs. She stopped at the top, crossing over onto firmer territory.

"Better?" I asked, coming up beside her alongside the railing.

She nodded. "Yeah. I thought I could handle the dock again, but it was too much. Ironically, I've probably inherited Declan's boat now that he's gone. I wish I could go out on it, but the only time I did, I started throwing up as soon as we left the dock. They had to immediately turn around and drop me off." She stared at the blank spot next to the dock that the boat had vacated. "Maybe Bill or Jared would want to buy it from me. Anyway, the wedding was wonderful. Sorry I was such a pill this week. I think what I need after this is some time to decompress and get away from all the memories of happier times with Declan."

"That sounds like a great idea." I smiled. "And don't worry about it. This has been a stressful time for everyone."

"Thanks." She surprised me by giving me a quick hug, then waved and walked away.

I stared blankly at the empty boat slip. I had a feeling this whole thing hinged on the boat. How and when had it arrived at the Boathouse's docks? Both Lindsay and Orson had mentioned the boat still being there when they went to bed. So Declan must have driven the truck and boat trailer out to the Ericksville boat launch after that point, then come back to the lake and somehow been hit in the head and launched into the lake. Or, alternatively, someone else had brought the boat and the body to our docks. After seeing Lindsay's extreme seasickness in person, I knew there was no way she could have taken the boat out by herself and piloted it over to the Boathouse's docks. However, I was becoming convinced that my second hypothesis was correct. I remembered seeing Daniel hiding the Lego man in his sailboat.

When I'd seen the boat at the lake house, it had been uncovered. But, when it was docked at the Boathouse, it had sported a red cover. Declan had loved his boat and hadn't wanted the pristine interior to be sullied by a seagull dive-bombing it. Much like Daniel with the Lego man, someone could have placed Declan's body in the boat and then used the covering to hide it while in transport.

But who? And why? His truck and boat trailer had been found in the boat launch parking area the morning I'd found his body. So if my theory was correct and the killer was one of Declan's friends staying at Lake Elinor, how had they returned to the lake house? I supposed they could have used a ride service, but then there would have been a record.

"Hey," Desi said, coming up behind me. "I'm leaving

now. I have to get home to feed Lina. Do you want me to come back when I'm done to help with anything?"

I shook my head. "No, I've got plenty of staff tonight. Go home."

She walked away, but before she reached the door, I called out to her, "Wait!"

She turned back to me. "Changed your mind?"

"No. But I did have a favor for you. Can you ask Tomàs if they checked the ride services in the area to see if anyone picked up a fare at the marina the night Declan died?"

"Sure. But why?"

"Well, if Declan was killed at Lake Elinor, someone must have transported his body to this area. I think whoever killed him hid his body in the boat, under the cover, so no one would see it on the way here."

She nodded slowly. "That makes sense. And if the police found Declan's truck and trailer at the Ericksville boat launch, how did the killer get back to Lake Elinor?"

"That's what I'm hoping to find out." I stared out at the docks again.

"I'll ask him." She gave me a quick hug and left.

Niely had written another article about the murder investigation for last week's paper, and we'd received several more cancellations over the last few days. Time was running out and I needed to solve this puzzle fast. Becca and Bill's friends would be leaving the lake house the next day, and without the wedding as an excuse, I'd have a hard time getting them to talk to me without raising their suspicions.

As if she'd read my mind, Desi called me the next morning, bright and early. I rolled over in bed to check the time—

seven o'clock. Adam was still sawing logs next to me. Ella had woken up at two, but I'd given her a bottle and she was out after that.

"Hey," I whispered.

"Are you still in bed?" Her voice blared over the phone, clearing the brain fog.

I closed my eyes for a moment. "Not anymore. Hold on." I swung my legs over the side of the bed, grabbed my bathrobe, and headed downstairs. When I was safely out of danger of waking up the rest of my family, I held the phone up to my ear again.

"Ok, sorry. I can talk now. Everyone was still asleep."

"Lucky." She yawned. "Lina woke up at five and hasn't napped since. Anthony heard her crying, and he demanded breakfast. Luckily, Tomàs wasn't working today, so he took care of the heart-shaped pancakes."

Pancakes sounded really good. I hadn't had much to eat last night during the reception because I'd been working, and now my stomach wasn't happy. I turned on the coffee pot and popped some bread into the toaster.

"Are you just calling me to complain, or did you need something?"

"Haha. Very funny. You haven't had your morning coffee yet, have you?"

"I just told you that you woke me up. So no, no coffee yet," I grumbled.

"You are grouchy without your morning caffeine." She laughed. "I was calling to see if you'd be interested in going out to Lake Elinor with me this morning."

"I guess I could. Why are you going out there? Becca won't be there."

"Yeah, I know," she said. "I wanted to say goodbye to Orson. We had some good talks when I visited with everyone at the lake house, and he's going back to California today. I didn't get a chance to talk with him last night because he didn't come back after Lindsay gave her toast and he chased after her."

"Why do you want me to come with?" Not that I was complaining. It was a prime means of interviewing everyone who remained at the house without raising too much suspicion.

She sighed dramatically. "Tomàs won't let me go by myself. He said with Declan's murderer still in the wind, he doesn't want me alone out there. So I thought you could come with me."

I could picture her pouting.

"Please?"

"Yeah, I can come with. What time?"

"I'm thinking I would pick you up at nine? Then we can be out there by ten. Everyone should still be there before they head home."

"Ok, but you're bringing me coffee."

"Deal." Desi hung up and I buttered my toast, carrying it and the cup of coffee with me over to the kitchen table. The solitude was nice. I'd been surrounded by people for the last week and having the house quiet was amazing.

It didn't last long. Ella started crying, then a cranky little boy came downstairs complaining about how annoying his baby sister was. Adam's voice came over the baby monitor in the living room as he soothed her.

In a few minutes, everyone was in the kitchen and the blissful silence was over. But I had my family together on a sunny Sunday morning. The world was looking up.

My mother had left early in the morning to return home to Idaho, so Adam made breakfast for himself and Mikey while I set Ella up in her highchair with a bottle and a tray full of Cheerios. When my husband was seated, I said, "Desi asked me to go out to Lake Elinor with her this morning. I should be back by noon though. Do you want to take the kids down to the beach? Maybe get some lunch at Elmer's Sea of Fish?"

"Sure." He opened the copy of the *Ericksville Times* that he'd retrieved from our front porch. The headline blared out, "Eleven days and the Boathouse Killer is still on the loose."

I groaned. Niely MacDonald and her sensationalist journalism. I pointed at the article. "The Boathouse Killer? Really? They need to get their facts straight. He wasn't even killed at the Boathouse." My shoulders tensed as I grew angrier. "They should call him the Lake Elinor Killer if anything."

"What's a killer?" Mikey asked innocently.

"Uh...nothing honey." I regretted my outburst, but Niely made me so mad.

"But what is it?" He peered up at me.

"I'll explain it to you later. Finish your Cheerios and then you can go play, ok?"

"Ok." Mikey dutifully put a spoonful of cereal in his mouth.

Adam looked up from the comics.

"The Lake Elinor Killer? As in where you're going with Desi today? That's where Desi's friend died?"

My eyes darted to Mikey's face, but he was engrossed in catching the Cheerios that floated in his bowl.

"Yes. I told you that."

"No, you told me that the man died in a lake. You didn't mention it happened to be where you've been spending so much time." He folded the newspaper closed and eyed me with concern.

"It's not a big deal. Desi is going with me. We'll be careful. It's the middle of the day. Who in their right mind would try anything in broad daylight?" I smiled at him, trying to convince him as much as myself. "Besides, Tomàs is ok with Desi going."

"Fine, but give me a call when you get there."

"I will." I gave him a peck on the cheek and cleared my breakfast dishes, stacking them in the sink because the dishwasher was full of clean dishes. "I'm going upstairs to shower and get ready to go."

Ella cried out because she'd run out of Cheerios, and Adam was too busy getting her more to respond to me.

20

$\mathcal{I}$ jumped into Desi's car as soon as she pulled up to the curb, before Adam could change his mind about me leaving.

Desi turned to me. "I told Tomàs about your theory that someone moved Declan's body in the boat. He seemed skeptical, but he called the station last night to ask them to check the local ride services."

"Ok. Did you hear anything back yet?" If they found something, this could break the case wide-open. I felt a little thrill that we could be so close to the end of this.

"They called Tomàs right before I left. Nothing. None of the ride services had picked up a customer anywhere near the Boathouse in the middle of the night, much less driven them all the way to Lake Elinor. Someone would have remembered that fare for sure."

My elation deflated. "Oh. Ok. Thanks for asking him." I'd been so sure I was right. If I wasn't right, how had Declan ended up in the Sound? I spent the rest of the ride to the lake trying to make sense of it.

When we arrived at Lake Elinor, I noticed that Declan's

boat was back already. It sat securely on the long boat trailer, which was hooked up to Declan's truck. The boat had been tucked away near the rear of the house and covered with its red cloth, ready to be driven down the road. I started to walk toward it.

"I'm going into the house to say goodbye to Orson, ok?" Desi shut her car door and walked purposefully toward the house.

I nodded. "I want to check something out on the boat. I'll be inside in a couple minutes."

"Ok," she called over her shoulder as she disappeared into the house.

I approached the boat. With it on the boat trailer, I couldn't really see much from the ground. I climbed onto the trailer and lifted the canvas cover. It was dark inside, and I couldn't see much. I looked around and didn't see anyone, so I dove into the boat.

It was pitch-black inside and, even after turning on the little penlight on my keychain, still really creepy. If this was how Declan's body had been transported from the lake to Puget Sound, there might be evidence in here. I shone the flashlight at all the little crevices inside the boat. The boat was clean, with nary a spot on the navy blue vinyl seat cushions. I pulled on the edge of one to help propel me further into the boat, toward the steering wheel.

The Velcro under it came loose under the force of my weight, shifting the cushion and revealing a reddish-brown smudge. I moved the light closer to it. It was definitely blood. In most boats, there would be the possibility that it was fish blood and not human. However, not in Declan's boat. I remembered how he'd been out there the first day I met him, diligently cleaning every nook and cranny of his boat. It was his prized possession, and he'd been fastidious about it. Whoever had cleaned this boat in the dark after dumping Declan's body had missed a spot. I snapped a photo of it with my phone to show the police later and texted it to Desi with the caption "Evidence!"

I scooted toward where I'd entered the boat and stuck my head out, then turtled back in when I heard footsteps.

"Yeah, I've got the boat. I'll meet you at the northbound rest stop off I-5, just north of Everton."

I froze. I recognized Jared's voice.

"Uh huh. The price is firm. Forty grand, just like I told you before. Don't try to scam me." He hung up and the foot-steps grew fainter.

When they stopped, I poked my head out, only to see Jared standing further down the drive, staring right at me.

"I thought I saw someone had messed with the cover, I just didn't figure it was you." He folded his arms across his chest.

"Uh, yeah. Lindsay told me she was thinking about selling the boat and my father-in-law was interested, so I was checking it out for him."

"Do you think I'm stupid?" He reached behind his back and, walking toward me, pulled a gun out of a back holster hidden beneath his shirt. He trained it on me. "I should have guessed you'd be the one to figure it out. You were always making up excuses to ask questions. Becca thought you were just interested in all of us, but I knew something was up."

"I *was* interested in everyone—you're Desi's friends and I wanted to get to know you better." My eyes were hypnotized by the barrel of the gun pointing straight at me. "That's all."

"Hmm..." he said, but his tone said he didn't believe me. "Well, it's too late now. I can't have you telling Lindsay that I stole her boat."

"It's not stolen, it's right here. I'm in it." I smiled winningly at him.

He gave me a withering look. "You know what I mean."

A rock rolled across the ground between us. Jared turned to see where it had come from, and I tried to make a break for it. Unfortunately, my foot caught on a rope inside the boat, and I was stuck. I wriggled my foot, but it wouldn't come out.

"Get in there with her," Jared said to whoever had caused the distraction.

I looked up. Desi stared guiltily at me. I sighed. Why had she come outside?

Then it hit me. I'd sent her the photo of the bloodstain. I was the reason she was now in danger.

He waved his gun at her, and she climbed inside the boat with me.

"Give me your phones. I don't want any calls for help."

We did as he asked and he pulled the covering tight across the back of the boat, sealing us in there.

"We're going for a little ride, ladies." He started up the truck and drove for only a few minutes before he began to back up. I heard a splash as the trailer tires hit water.

"Desi, we're in Lake Elinor," I whispered. She didn't answer.

She was sitting next to me on the floor of the boat, her breathing growing louder and faster. "Chocolate éclairs, cherry Danishes, walnut brownies, caramel squares. Chocolate éclairs, cherry Danishes—"

"Desi," I interrupted her. "He's putting the boat in the water. We've got to get out of here."

"Chocolate éclairs, cherry Danishes..." she continued reciting.

What was she doing? Then it hit me. Desi had severe

claustrophobia. She'd told me that one time she'd accidentally locked herself in a small closet at work and passed out
from anxiety. Luckily, one of the staff had needed something
from the closet, or she might not have been found for a
while.

Ok. Desi wasn't going to be much help as long as we
were stuck inside the covered boat. I racked my brain. What
could we do to get out of this situation? I tugged on the
covering, but it was tightly secured.

The boat continued to back up into the water. Was he
going to back the whole truck into the lake? When it felt like
the boat was starting to float, he stopped. I shivered despite
the warm weather and the stifling heat under the red
canvas.

Jared released the bindings on the canvas and pulled it
aside in front to allow him to get into the captain's seat. I
blinked at the glaring light that invaded our dark cave. Desi
tried to stand under the canvas, gasping for air near the
opening.

The gun poked under the canvas, nudging her back onto
the floor. "Sit down," he barked.

"You're not going to get away with this," I shouted.

"Really? Because I did with Declan." He backed the boat
completely off the trailer then spun it around to face out
into the lake. The motor roared as he zipped out to the
middle.

He yanked the cover off our heads. Desi's face was white
and her eyes panicked. I had to figure some way to get us out
of there. But how? We were in the middle of a lake, and all
the other boaters were down at the widest part of the lake,
too far away to hear a call for help.

"Declan found out from the business valuation that
someone had been draining the dental practice's bank

accounts, didn't he? He knew it was most likely one of his partners, but how did he find out it was you? Did he discover your gambling addiction?"

Jared's mouth twisted, turning his handsome face into a terrifying one. "He suspected, but he didn't confront me until early last week. I of course told him he was crazy. But then we got stuck rooming together, and he overheard me talking to my bookie. It was hard to get out of that. He said he'd give me a week to make it right, but there was no way I could return all the money I'd taken. It was gone."

"So you killed him to hide your embezzlement."

"I couldn't let him turn me in. I'd go to jail for sure if he and Bill pressed charges. I decided I'd have to get rid of him sometime during the week, and his fight with Lindsay at the rehearsal dinner gave me the perfect opportunity. He was so drunk, all I had to do was hit him over the head with an oar and then hold him under the water. I threw some beer bottles on the dock at the Boathouse so everyone would think he'd fallen into the water in a drunken stupor." He frowned. "I should have done it in the Sound, and then no one would have ever suspected."

"So it was premeditated," I said slowly. Color had returned to Desi's face, and she was listening intently to our conversation.

"I didn't have a choice." He cut the engine and turned to us. "Just like I don't have a choice now."

"What are you going to do to us?" Desi asked.

"You and your friend are going to have a horrible boating accident. I'll set someone's rowboat free on the lake, so they'll think you went out on it and drowned."

I glanced at the far-off lakeshore. From this distance, the boats and kayaks looked like miniatures dotting the sand in front of the houses. There was only water surrounding us. There would be no rescue from any outside party.

I needed to know. "So how did you get back to Lake Elinor after you dumped the boat and Declan's body?"

He smiled smugly. "I'd left my car in the long-term parking by the ferry. Easy enough to walk over there and retrieve it, then tell everyone the car dealership had delivered it early that morning." He leaned over the front seat to pull the remaining canvas off the boat, fighting with it with his right hand to unhook it. His left hand trained the gun on us as he threw the canvas over our heads. "Now, time for you two to have an unfortunate accident."

I saw Desi reach into her pocket, then her eyes widened and she yelled, "Watch out!"

Out of nowhere, a speedboat towing a water skier flew past us, going way too fast. Their wake rocked our boat and water splashed aboard. Desi and I were still on the floor, so we didn't get jostled too much, but the force of the waves threw Jared off-kilter. He lost his balance on the side of the boat, and Desi took that opportunity to throw something in his face. He rubbed his eyes with the hand he'd used to brace himself, howling in pain as tears streamed down his face.

Another wave jolted the boat and he lurched forward, smacking his head with a sickening crunch on the side of the boat, and then, as if in slow motion, slid off the boat like a sea lion diving into the ocean.

Desi and I exchanged glances before we both stumbled to our feet and rushed over to the edge.

"I don't see anything." Desi peered into the water.

"Me neither," I said grimly. Although Jared had been about to kill us, I didn't want him to drown.

"I hate to say it, but it seems fitting, considering what he did to Declan." Desi's voice held a note of shock, and she was shivering despite the heat.

I turned in a slow circle, scanning the water for signs of life. There were none. "We should go back to the house."

Desi nodded. "I think he left our cell phones in the truck." She cast another glance at the water, then climbed into the captain's seat and started the motor.

The closer the boat got to dry land, the better I felt. When we got to the shore, we tied up to someone's dock and walked through some tall grass to the truck. The trailer was still in the water, and the vehicle was unlocked. Jared hadn't been expecting to be gone long. I shuddered, remembering his body slipping under the water. We'd come too close to dying ourselves.

I grabbed my cell phone, which was sitting on the passenger seat, and called the police. When they showed up, they gave us blankets to wrap around our shoulders and told us to sit on a bench nearby while they investigated.

Desi and I huddled together with our blankets on. A cloud had blocked the sun, causing the temperature to drop by at least twenty degrees.

"Do you think they'll find him?" I asked. A police boat had been dispatched to the center of the lake, but nothing had turned up yet.

"I don't know. Probably not. Lake Elinor is a glacial lake and has some pretty deep trenches. They may never find him." She stared out at the boat in the middle of the lake, which from this distance looked as small as the one Mikey had made at Sail Away camp.

"We could have died out there. That could have been us." I wrapped the blanket tighter around me.

"I know." She swiped at her eyes.

"What was that you threw at him anyways?"

"Glitter," she said matter-of-factly.

"You just happened to have glitter in your pocket?" It had done the trick nicely though.

"Remember the paintings they did at camp of their dream boat? The ones where they could glue stuff on?"

"Yeah, why?"

"Well, Anthony wanted glitter on his, but he ran out of time. He wouldn't let me leave without having Ms. Shana put some glitter in a bag for him to add at home. I stuck it in my pocket and forgot it was there until we were in the boat." She laughed. "Good thing I didn't stick them in the washing machine with the glitter in the pocket. That would be a mess."

I shook my head. Sometimes the peculiar items that get shoved at moms every day could come in handy. "Well, good thing you had it."

"Ms. Andrews? Ms. Torres? We're ready for you now." A young, female police officer led us over to where they'd set up a mobile command post.

We told them that Jared had been responsible for Declan's death and how he'd done it. After they took our statements and released us, a policeman escorted us back to Becca's lake house in his patrol car.

We stood outside the lake house, unsure of what to do.

"Should we tell them?" Desi asked, almost in a whisper.

I glanced up at the living room windows. I didn't see anyone, but all the cars were still there. I sighed. "Yeah, let's go."

We told Lindsay and then Orson about what had

happened to Jared. Orson sat down heavily on the sofa and put his head in his hands.

Looking up, he said, "I can't believe this. Jared? He's one of my best friends... and Declan's too." His face was ashen.

Desi went over to him and sat down next to him, wrapping her arm around his shoulders. "I know. If I hadn't been there, I wouldn't have believed it either." She blanched a little thinking of our recent experience out on the lake.

"Are you all right?" Orson asked, glancing between Desi and me.

I nodded. "We're ok, just a little shaken up. Actually, we'd better get home. We weren't supposed to be out here for so long, and our families will be worried about us."

Desi stood. "You'll tell Becca and Bill, right? I'd hate for them to hear about it from the police." Her voice held unshed tears.

"We will," Lindsay said. Orson just closed his eyes.

"I'll call you later," Desi promised.

We got into the car and sat there for a moment, both of us gazing out at the lake.

"It doesn't even seem real," I said.

"I know." The tears began to flow out of Desi's eyes. "What happened to Jared to make him like that? He was always such a nice, fun-loving guy back in college."

"I don't know." I leaned over in the front seat to give her a quick hug. "It may have been a gambling addiction, or something else entirely. We'll never know."

"I guess not." Desi wiped her tears away and, without a look back, drove us away from Lake Elinor for the last time.

21

A little over a week later, everything was getting back to normal—in my life and at the Boathouse. Beth was back at work but had decided to cut back on some of her hours so that she could concentrate on her health. She'd offered to hire someone else to help take the extra workload off of me, but I'd deferred that decision for another month.

"Jill, can you please go through the voicemails from last night? The requests for new bookings are coming in faster than I can contact the potential clients." Beth lowered herself into her chair and rested her arms on the desk.

"I can go through them this morning." I scanned her face. She looked exhausted. "Do you need me to get you anything? Water? Coffee?"

Beth motioned to the cups on her desk. "Nope, I'm all set. Thanks though."

"Sure, no problem." I turned to leave.

"Hey, Jill," she said.

I turned back around.

"Thank you for everything you did for the Boathouse

while Lincoln and I were out of commission. We both really appreciate it."

"Of course. But next time, do you think you could choose a time to have heart surgery that isn't in the middle of a murder investigation?" I teased.

She laughed. "I'll do my best. And better yet, maybe you can stay out of the middle of murder investigations." She raised her eyebrows at me, then pulled a file out of a drawer and laid it open on the desk. "Even with the bookings that were canceled during that time period, we're still looking good. People snapped up those dates when they found out they'd become available. I guess what they say is true—any publicity is good publicity."

I remembered how it felt to have the reporters congregating outside, hungry for any tidbit to make their next story. "I don't know about that, but I'm glad it turned out ok in the end." I left her office and returned to mine, determined to get through all of the voicemails and e-mails before lunchtime. I'd made plans to meet Desi for a walk at lunchtime, and I needed to go home and relieve Adam of Ella-duty before meeting her at the café.

When I got to the café, I wheeled the stroller inside. Desi was standing behind the counter with Lina, bouncing her lightly as she shifted from foot to foot.

"Hey. Let me just tell Andrea that I'm leaving. Oh, and I have news."

"Good or bad?"

Her face darkened. "A little of both."

What did she have to tell me? I'd seen her briefly the day before, so it was something new. By the time she rolled up with Lina's stroller, I'd worked myself up wondering about her news.

"What did you need to tell me?" I asked as soon as we were clear of the café.

"Tomàs called me at work today." She paused for dramatic effect. "They found Jared's body. It washed ashore last night."

"Oh." Now I could see why she'd said both good and bad news. I was happy to have closure but hearing that they'd found his body made his death so final. I knew it wasn't our fault that he had died, but it still brought up bad feelings.

"Yeah. That's pretty much how I felt. I keep asking myself if I hadn't thrown the glitter at him, would he have hit his head and fallen in the water? I can't get that image of him sinking out of my head."

"He was going to kill us. I think you acted in self-defense. And it could have been solely the force of the wake that knocked him over. We don't know."

"But still..."

"Anything you did was done to save our lives and it worked. We're here, with our babies, enjoying the sun. Let's try to put this out of our heads now, ok?" I knew it was easier said than done, but I wanted to try to forget. "It feels good to get outside and exercise a little." I held on to the stroller handles and leaned forward to stretch my hamstrings. Although I'd vowed to establish a more regular exercise regime this summer, all of that had gone by the wayside when I realized how busy work would be in the summer season.

Desi laughed. "I'm joining a gym after Labor Day. Pretty soon it will be back to rain in these parts."

She held her face up to the sun and closed her eyes. Lina cried, snapping her out of it. She pulled the stroller shade over Lina's face, and I did the same with Ella's stroller. We walked along side by side, enjoying the last days of summer. Not for the first time, I reflected on how lucky I was to have a job that allowed me the flexibility to spend so much time with my kids. I knew not everyone had that luxury.

We passed by the marina and a boat like Declan's caught my eye. Desi saw what I was looking at.

"Yeah, every time I see a boat now, I get a little claustrophobic. I honestly thought we were going to die in there." She leaned down to check on her baby.

"Me too." I changed the subject, at least partially. "Have you heard from Becca since the wedding?"

She brightened. "I did. She and Bill had a wonderful time on the island at some place that offers luxury cabins right on the beach." Laughing, she said, "I keep dropping hints to Tomàs that it would be nice for our anniversary, but I'm not sure it's getting through to him."

"And the dental practice? Is Bill alone there now, or did he hire another partner?" With both Declan and Jared dead, it must be strange for him there.

"Oh. I forgot I hadn't told you about that. Becca said he's going to sell the practice, and they're going to move to San Francisco. There were too many memories for him here. It was weird enough for me to have Declan murdered and Jared try to kill us, and I wasn't even that close to them. It must be horrible for Bill."

"San Francisco? Did Becca take that tenure-track position?"

"She did." Desi smiled. "She told Bill about it, and after they got the news about Jared while on their honeymoon, they decided it was time for a fresh start."

"That's fantastic. I'm happy for her. For them both." We stopped at a spot next to the beach. I closed my eyes and let the salty air enter my lungs. A soft breeze blew my hair back, but the warmth of the late August sun kept it from being chilly.

"Me too."

We turned around for the walk back toward the Boathouse and café. Soon, the days would get shorter and the rain would come, but for now, I was going to soak up all the sun that I could. At the Boathouse, I waved goodbye to Desi and brought Ella into my office. The new babysitter, Rachel, was scheduled to meet me there for a trial run. I'd introduced her to the kids last week, and she and Mikey had become fast friends.

Rachel got to the Boathouse at one o'clock on the dot and took Ella out for another walk. I didn't get much work done though, because Adam showed up soon after that.

"Have you had a chance to eat yet?" He had an odd smile on his face, but I couldn't tell what it meant.

"No, not really." I'd eaten some string cheese and crackers, but my lunch break had been used to go walking with Desi.

"Let's get takeout from Elmer's."

We walked over to Elmer's to get fish and chips and ate them at one of the picnic tables outside. When we finished, Adam grabbed our paper baskets and threw them in the trash, then held out his hand to me. "I want to show you something."

I took his hand and gazed into his eyes. He was up to something. "What is it?"

"You'll see," he said mysteriously. He led me up a block from the water and a few streets over, stopping in front of a two-story brick building next to an ophthalmologist's office.

"Ok. Why are we here?" Although it was well-kept, I didn't see anything special about the building.

He walked to the flowerbeds near the door and reached

behind a large bush, pulling out a rectangular object about a foot long and six inches wide.

"Ta-da!" he said, presenting it to me with a flourish.

I turned it over. "Adam Andrews, Attorney at Law."

He beamed at me.

I stared up at him and pointed at the door. "This is yours? You signed a lease?" Hope zinged through me. Was this really happening?

He nodded. "Tomorrow is my last day at the firm. Brenda really came through with this one. I think she may have been working overtime on finding me something because she mentioned how grateful she was for your support when she needed it."

I started to cry and threw my arms around him. His muscles tensed up, and he patted me on the back.

"Honey, it's ok. Everything will work out." He seemed to think I was worried about money or something.

"No, no. I'm happy." I pulled back from him, wiping my eyes, and my mouth spread into a huge smile. "These are happy tears."

"Well, good. I know this has been a long time coming."

I rubbed my fingers over the raised letters on the sign. Maybe it wasn't completely a fresh start, but this was a new chapter in our lives, and I was excited to start reading it.

AUTHOR'S NOTE

*T*hank you for reading A Deadly Pair O'Docks! I hope you enjoyed spending more time with Jill Andrews and her family. If you did, I'd really appreciate it if you left a review.

For information about my new releases and other exciting news, please visit my website, nicoleellisauthor.com and sign up for my e-mail newsletter.

If you'd like to read more about Jill and her family, read Book #4, Stuck with S'More Death.

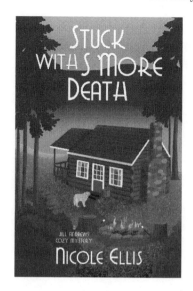

Books by Nicole Ellis

<u>Jill Andrews Cozy Mysteries</u>
>Brownie Points for Murder (Book 1)
Death to the Highest Bidder (Book 2)
A Deadly Pair O'Docks (Book 3)
Stuck with S'More Death (Book 4)
Murderous Mummy Wars (Book 5)
A Killer Christmas Party (Book 6)

<u>Candle Beach Sweet Romances</u>
>Sweet Beginnings (Book 1)
Sweet Success (Book 2)
Sweet Promises (Book 3)

Sweet Memories (Book 4)
Sweet History (Book 5)
Sweet Matchmaking (Book 6)

Made in the USA
Coppell, TX
26 April 2020